MIXED-
MARRIAGE
DAUGHTER

MIXED-MARRIAGE DAUGHTER

by Hila Colman

WILLIAM MORROW AND COMPANY NEW YORK

This book is for
JENNIFER,
ETHAN,
SUSAN,
and BENJAMIN.

MIXED-
MARRIAGE
DAUGHTER

I

How can I stand to move away from New York! The thought panicked Sophie as she walked up Fifth Avenue, her blond hair streaming in the wind, only half-conscious of the admiring glances given her long, shapely legs appearing below her very brief skirt. "It will be like saying good-bye to a lover," she said aloud to Abbie, her friend walking beside her. Since Sophie was barely seventeen and her knowledge of lovers rather skimpy, she giggled at her own phrase.

"But I do love New York," she said emphatically, "and I loathe the idea of living in a small town."

"It may not be so bad," Abbie said unconvincingly. "Some of these suburbs are pretty wild."

"Woodview, Massachusetts, is not a suburb. It is a small town. I don't think it's even very near Boston." Sophie's face was woebegone. "I am going to hate it," she said firmly. She took a deep breath. "I love this poisonous air, I love the smell, I love the stores, I love the people on the streets, I even love the subway. Can you imagine walking down Main Street on a Saturday afternoon?"

"Don't be silly," Abbie said. "You'll be going to football games and parties. I'm sure your parents will join a country club—with fabulous dances."

Sophie didn't answer. She doubted very much that her parents would join a country club. They weren't the type. Her father was a schoolteacher, and they were moving to Woodview because he was taking a job as the principal of the grade school. Her mother put country clubs in the same category as bridge and golf, both of which she considered foolish pastimes for women who had nothing better to do.

"Some of those country places in New England are divine," Abbie chatted on. "I was invited to a house party once that was out of this world. We moved from house to house and never got to bed at all. Finally we all went swimming in somebody's pool, and then the boy I was with put a huge dent in his father's Jaguar. He was so scared to go home he spent the day with me. He was terrific. His father's president of some big oil company."

As always Sophie was fascinated by these glimpses into Abbie's life. Abbie was the richest girl she had ever known. Her father had a seat on the Stock Exchange, she lived in a large apartment on upper Fifth Avenue, and she was brought to school in a long, chauffeur-driven Cadillac.

Other things about Abbie intrigued Sophie too. Abbie was Society with a capital S. She was going to be a debutante and have a coming-out party at a fashionable hotel, her father played polo, and her mother's picture often appeared in the society pages of the newspapers. Sophie was amused that they were friends although they came from such different worlds.

Most of the girls who attended Sophie's exclusive, private school were more or less in Abbie's class. Rich and protected. Sophie was there only because her father was an educator and had managed a scholarship for her. "I hope it doesn't make a snob of you," Sophie's mother had said, but Sophie pooh-poohed the notion.

The thought of leaving her school made Sophie want to weep. "I think it's mean to have to change schools now, just before my senior year," she said to Abbie. "I won't be graduating with anyone I know!"

"You'll make friends up there," Abbie said consolingly.

What Sophie didn't say was that on top of everything else she hated the idea of graduating from an ordinary small-town public school instead of from the Beardsley School for Girls. It would give her an entirely different status at college. Her mother would call that concern being snobbish, but she didn't care. Facts were facts, and Sophie often thought that she was more worldly than her mother.

The girls parted at Fifty-seventh Street. Sophie took a bus up to Riverside Drive where she lived, and Abbie took a taxi to her home.

On the bus, Sophie became more and more depressed. From her point of view, her father couldn't have picked a more awkward time to take a new job. What could be worse than changing schools right before her senior year, leaving all her friends? Furthermore, they were moving

14

from a big city where there was everything to a small town where there was nothing. Sophie knew enough about Woodview to be sure that it had absolutely no relation to the New England that Abbie had visited.

Sophie's mother, Mrs. Barnes, came from Woodview. She had been born and brought up there, and Sophie's maternal grandparents, Ma and Pa Golden, and her aunts and uncles lived there. Through them Mr. Barnes had heard about the job opening. On the few occasions that Sophie had visited Woodview she had seen enough to gather that it was a deadly town, where the girls wore their hair too short and their skirts too long. Although she hadn't been there for a few years she was sure it hadn't changed.

Her parents were happy about the idea of getting away from the city. Mr. Barnes was excited by the prospect of being the principal of a rural school, and her mother seemed to be looking forward to the move as some kind of special reunion with her parents and the rest of her family. As far as she had known, her mother had rather enjoyed living in a big city, and Sophie couldn't understand why anyone would want to leave it for a small town. The geography didn't matter, Mrs. Barnes had explained; she was going home, home to her family.

Little by little, Sophie had begun to understand certain

things she had never thought about before. She had never paid particular attention to the fact that her parents represented a mixed marriage—one Gentile, one Jew—and because they had a good marriage the realization had not dawned on her that at one time it had presented a problem. But recently, from things Mrs. Barnes said, she realized that her mother must have caused some kind of an explosion by leaving Woodview to marry a Gentile boy and that there had been a rift in the family. Now when her mother spoke of going back to Woodview, tears came into her eyes and she grew both apprehensive and eager. She seemed to have to reassure herself continually by saying things such as, "Everything will be all right after all these years. It will be wonderful to show off my beautiful daughter and my handsome husband," adding a nervous little laugh. "We should be more tolerant now that all of us are older, and I'm sure no one wants to dig up old wounds."

Sophie thought that her mother's wanting to show her off was funny. "As if I were something you'd bought in a department store," she said.

But if the move was all right for her parents, it was all wrong for her. Sophie stared out of the bus window at the Hudson River and let the depression envelop her. New York had never looked so beautiful; the park along the

Drive was bright with late summer colors, and the sun setting behind the Palisades was turning everything to gold. If there were only some way she could stay in the city. . . .

Suddenly she had an idea, and she could barely wait to reach her stop. Off the bus, she went flying into her house and was relieved to find her mother at home. "I've got a brainstorm," Sophie cried with excitement. "Why couldn't I stay in the city and live with Grandma and Grandpa Barnes?"

Sophie was very fond of her father's parents and visited them in their old-fashioned brownstone on Brooklyn Heights whenever she could. She loved the large rooms with their high ceilings and brick fireplaces, the beautiful view of the East River and Manhattan, but most of all she liked the atmosphere. There was a quiet, shabby elegance to the house that appealed to her: dark mahogany furniture, old silver, and waxed floors. Often she found her grandmother painstakingly working on an embroidered replica of the Barnes family tree. Sophie liked the idea that on one side of her family her ancestors had settled in America over two hundred years ago. In fact, a Franklin Barnes had established a church in Virginia and had a tiny village named after him.

When the opportunity arose, she was fond of saying

that her grandfather was a retired Congregational minister, even though she rarely, if ever, mentioned that she was also the granddaughter of Sam Golden, who owned a clothing store in Woodview, Massachusetts. There was little doubt in her mind that being the granddaughter of a minister had more style than being one of a man who had started out life as a salesman—a peddler, he called it—of men's underwear. She considered her idea of living with the elder Barnes a brilliant suggestion.

Her mother, however, was not enthusiastic. "Your father and I want you with us," Mrs. Barnes said. "After all you'll be going away to college next year. Besides, we think the change will be good for you. You know we haven't liked these society girls you've been going around with. They're a pretty shallow bunch."

"That's ridiculous," Sophie said indignantly. "You sent me to this school, and I'd like to graduate with my class. That's only reasonable."

"I know." Mrs. Barnes was trying to be sympathetic. "But I think you'll like Woodview. You've never lived in a small town, and the young people in one can have a very good time. It will be a new and healthy experience for you."

"I expect I'll hate it," Sophie said with conviction.

"Why don't you wait till you get there before you make

up your mind?" her mother suggested. "Don't judge it beforehand. I know this move is hard on you, but I think you'll be glad that you had the year there. There's a great big world outside of New York."

"A deadly one," Sophie said morosely. She could tell from her mother's face that there was no point in arguing further.

II

The house in Woodview lived up to Sophie's worst expectations. "It's dull and uninteresting," Sophie decided promptly.

"It's a perfectly good house," Mr. Barnes said calmly. Her father was a tall, sandy-haired man, who looked younger than his forty-two years. "It's solidly built, plenty of light, the rooms are big enough. . . . What more do you want?"

Mrs. Barnes answered for Sophie. "She wants *charm.* Some broken-down old house with creaky plumbing and dust-catching nooks and crannies. Either that or something frightfully modern."

"It has no style. It looks like every other white clapboard house on the block, except that it has a porch on the side instead of the front."

"Well, it's not your house; it's ours. We had to take what we could get. When you have your own house, you can suit yourself." Mrs. Barnes was looking at the furniture piled up in the room. "I think it's going to be all right when we get straightened out," she said.

Sophie went upstairs to examine her room again. It was in the back of the house overlooking a small lawn and garden with a tall shade tree that kept out the afternoon sun. She could see the backyard and the back of the house on the next street. The house, the street, the yard represented everything she despised. They all were mediocre and banal, she thought, deciding that she preferred to be either very rich or very poor, but not in between.

When Sophie went out to explore the town, she found it even more depressing. It was a hot Saturday afternoon in late August. Main Street in Woodview looked like a ghost town. It was bare of trees, and the blistering sun on the sidewalks made Sophie's feet burn through her thin sandals. The corner drugstore was deserted, except for a few teen-age, long-haired, aimless-looking boys standing outside with bored expressions on their pimply faces. They stared at Sophie with a listless curiosity that made her feel that they were no more interested in her than she in them.

The stores were drab. A jewelry store, a hardware store, a shoe store—one looked less interesting than the next. A girl in shorts came out of the shoe store with her hair done up in dozens of pink curlers. The movie theater had a film that Sophie had seen two years before. She couldn't help but think of her Saturday afternoon walk with Abbie up Fifth Avenue a few weeks back. What a contrast!

Sophie didn't think she would survive the year she had to live here before going away to college.

Then she turned the corner, and there was Golden's Clothing Store facing her. The big sign startled her. The store had changed since she last had seen it several years before. A new modern front, with angular show windows and lots of shiny chrome had been put in. One side displayed men's clothes, and the other women's. The women's side showed girls' back-to-school clothes: jumpers and sweaters and skirts.

Sophie thought that both the clothes and the new front were hideous, and yet standing there, staring at the windows, she was filled with a strange emotion. She found the attempt to make the store attractive oddly touching, but the knowledge that the people responsible were her family was embarrassing. How could anyone connected with her have such dreadful taste?

Quickly she turned away from the store, terrified that someone who knew her might see her. She hurried down the street and back home.

It was late afternoon when Sophie placed her last book on the shelf. She surveyed the room critically. Her own things made it look better, and there were still plenty to add. She had to make curtains, put up her posters on the wall, and do some painting. One wall, she thought, could be orange, and she could get an orange bedspread. . . .

"Sophie, are you ready?" Her father's voice called from downstairs. "It's time to leave."

"Yes, I'll be down." And then she added wistfully, foolishly, "I suppose I have to come?"

"Of course, you have to come," her father said impatiently. When she came downstairs, her mother's face was unhappy.

"I'm tired of that long face of yours," Mrs. Barnes said. "The whole family will be at Grandma's to welcome us, and you had better make up your mind to be agreeable.

You're behaving in the most spoiled, outrageous fashion."

"I'm sorry," Sophie said helplessly. "But I can't pretend to be happy when I'm not. I'm not an actress."

"You can at least make an effort," Mr. Barnes told her. "You don't have to give in to your moods so indulgently, you know."

"Giving me a lecture isn't going to help," Sophie remarked. "You hung this hall mirror too low," she said to her mother, glancing at herself in it.

"Never mind the mirror. Come on." Mrs. Barnes walked out of the house, and Sophie and her father followed.

The Goldens lived in a big house on a hill overlooking the town. "It used to be beautiful up here when I was young," Mrs. Barnes said with a sad note in her voice, as they drove up the hill. "Nothing but woods and some open fields where cows grazed. Now it's all built up."

"With terrible developments," Sophie commented.

"They're not pretty," Mrs. Barnes agreed. The hillside was dotted with tiny pink, yellow, and white houses, all alike and bare of trees in their small yards.

"Why didn't your mother and father move?" Sophie asked. "I'd hate to look down on this."

"They wouldn't dream of moving. It's their home. We

24

all grew up in that house. Besides, they have four acres so they're off by themselves." She seemed shocked at the idea of her parents moving.

"I grew up in our apartment, but you thought moving from it was all right," Sophie said.

"A house is different," Mrs. Barnes said, closing her lips firmly, an indication that she didn't want to get into that discussion again.

There were several cars parked outside of the Goldens' house, and the porch was filled with people. To Sophie they all seemed to be talking at once.

"Sophie, you've grown so. I wouldn't know you!" She was being hugged by her Grandmother Dora. Mrs. Golden was a small, pretty, plump woman, whose graying hair was dyed a jet black. She was well corseted in a brightly printed, sleeveless dress that set off her tanned skin and made her look like an animated summer bouquet. She moved quickly, hugging Sophie, hugging Mrs. Barnes, and getting up on her toes to kiss her son-in-law.

"Welcome, welcome to Woodview. This is the happiest day of my life, to have the whole family, *almost* the whole family together. Sophie, darling, you're even prettier than before. Come, sweetheart, you have to meet everyone."

25

She took Sophie's hand and was about to lead her onto the screened porch.

"Dora, your soup is burning." Mr. Golden spoke with more resignation than urgency. "I told you not to make soup on such a hot day."

"Oh, my!" Mrs. Golden sniffed the air, which was unmistakably filled with the odor of burning food. "My borsch, my borsch. . . ." She flew into the kitchen, but reappeared in a few minutes flushed and triumphant. "It's all right, Sam," she said soothingly. "It just spilled over a little on the burner. He always likes to get something on me." She patted his bald head affectionately. "Poor Sam, he has a terrible wife."

"Ach, everyone should have such a wife." Mr. Golden had the deadpan face of a natural stooge. It was a long face, with a prominent nose, that carried a perpetually melancholy expression, yet in his small eyes and twisted mouth an impish humor lurked. "She forgets everything. Sometimes she forgets who her husband is. The other night, all of a sudden, she calls me Nathan. Who is Nathan?" Mr. Golden shrugged his shoulders. He was a short, stocky man, about the same height as his wife. Leaning forward, he kissed her on the cheek. "Nathan she called me. . . ."

Mrs. Golden laughed merrily. "He'll never let me forget it. I was talking to our accountant on the phone. His name is Nathan, so when I hang up I call Sam, Nathan, by mistake. So now he thinks I have Nathan on the brain. You should see him, a little skinny runt of a man. I wouldn't have him if you gave him to me. Come on, everybody's waiting to see you." She took Sophie's hand again.

Sophie had waited for her grandparents while her mother and father had gone around to the screened porch to join the others. Sophie was a little embarrassed by her grandparents. In all the years she had known Mother and Father Barnes, she didn't think she had ever seen them kiss, and she had certainly never heard them talk this way.

Sophie's mother was the middle child between two brothers, and Sophie's two aunts and uncles were now waiting to greet her. She was kissed effusively by Aunt Helen and Uncle Abe, and Aunt Sara and Uncle Harry. Abe and Harry were in the business with their father, and so they and their families lived in Woodview. The children of Uncle Abe, the older brother, were grown up and married and moved away, but Uncle Harry had a daughter, Rachel, two years younger than Sophie, and a twelve-year-old son, Dickie. Rachel was a shy, thin girl wearing what Sophie immediately marked as an unbecoming haircut. Rachel greeted Sophie with an eager smile.

"Where's Dickie?" Sophie asked, pleased with herself for remembering.

"Dickie's at camp," Aunt Sara told her.

Mrs. Golden looked around the room with a big smile of contentment on her face. "All my children together, and almost all my grandchildren. Only Joseph is missing. I begged him to come, but you know Joseph." She shrugged her plump shoulders. "He is a hermit, a real hermit."

Sophie tried to recall Uncle Joseph. He was actually her great uncle, since he was her grandmother's brother, but everyone in the family except his sister called him uncle. She had only seen him once or twice when she was little. Uncle Joseph had been in a concentration camp in Germany, and Sophie remembered being very frightened of him. He had looked like a skeleton, with a dark beard and sunken glowering eyes, and he had said very little. When he had tried clumsily to hug her as a child, she had been afraid. She had run to her mother crying, and her mother had scolded her. Uncle Joseph lived in a small house by himself just outside of town and worked on his inventions. No one in the family knew exactly what they were, but everyone was happy to contribute to his small income and to let him do what he wanted.

"Come, come, it's time to eat." Grandma Dora led her brood into the dining room, where there was a large dining table and a massive sideboard laden with silver. Rachel hovered near Sophie and sat down beside her.

Mrs. Golden brought a huge tureen of steaming soup to the table. "Even on a hot day it's good to have something warm in the stomach. In India they eat hot food all the time. After the soup you can have cold food."

Sophie couldn't keep up with all the conversations, and she gave up trying. Everyone was talking at once, and no one appeared to be listening. Her mother was chatting with Sophie's aunts; her father was discussing politics with the men. The babble seemed deafening.

"I hope you'll like it here. I've only been to New York a couple of times, but I don't know how anyone can live there." Rachel spoke to Sophie softly.

"I was thinking the opposite this afternoon when I walked around Woodview. It doesn't look like much fun," Sophie said.

"Well, I guess it would seem kind of dead to a New Yorker. A nice bunch of Jewish kids live in Worcester, and we go to the Community Center there a lot. It's part of the temple." Rachel spoke defensively.

"But what do you do in Woodview?" Sophie didn't want to say that she didn't think much of sectarian community centers.

"It's different in Woodview." Rachel spoke hesitantly. "There aren't many Jewish kids. I don't know what the others do. I guess some of them go to dances at the country club. A lot of them just ride around in their cars and go to the movies."

Sophie looked at her in astonishment. "You mean the Jewish kids don't mix with the others?"

"Of course not. Don't misunderstand me," Rachel added hastily. "We all get along. But we go our own ways. I mean you wouldn't want to date a Gentile boy. If you started liking each other, it could lead to a lot of trouble."

"But that's the most ridiculous thing I ever heard." Sophie was shocked. "If you really liked each other, what difference would it make?"

Rachel was embarrassed. "I suppose it's different for you, because of your mother and father. Everyone says that Aunt Esther and Uncle Peter are a rare exception. Grandma still gets tears in her eyes, though, when she talks about them. She asks what did she do wrong that that should have happened to her." Rachel flushed and added apologetically, "I guess I shouldn't have said that."

"It's all right," Sophie said unsmilingly. A wave of anger made her body tense up. She looked across the table at her father speaking quietly and authoritatively to the men. Sophie was positive he was the one who had all the right answers. Those men had to respect his ideas. How dare they look down on him because he was a Gentile! They were clothing salesmen, and he was a teacher, a principal. . . . The fury of her resentment made her put down her spoon and turn away from her unfinished bowl of soup.

Grandma Dora's sharp eye caught Sophie's gesture. "What's the matter, darling? You don't like my borsch?"

"It's delicious," Sophie said politely. She picked up the piece of rye bread on her plate and looked around the table. "Could I have some butter, please?"

Mrs. Golden's plump face was startled, and her smile froze. She glanced from her granddaughter to her daughter. The conversation at the table suddenly stopped. "In this house we don't eat butter with meat," Grandma Golden said in a clear, distinct voice. "Didn't anyone ever tell you about a kosher house?"

Mrs. Barnes's face was flushed. "Mama, she forgot. After all. . . ."

31

"After all, what?" Mrs. Golden demanded. "My own granddaughter should sit at my table and ask for butter. It's enough to make an old woman want to sit down and cry."

"Mama, don't get so upset." Her son Harry looked at Sophie sympathetically. "The kid made a mistake. It's not so terrible. I guess you'll have to eat your bread without butter," he said to Sophie with a little laugh.

"I'm sorry," Sophie spoke to her grandmother apologetically. "I suppose I should have known, but I really didn't. You'll have to forgive me. After all," she added with a smile, "I'm only half-Jewish."

"Half-Jewish!" Mrs. Golden's face was shocked. "Half-Jewish!" she repeated with contempt. "Your mother's Jewish. By Jewish law if your mother's Jewish, you're Jewish. You'll have to forgive me, Peter," she said to her son-in-law, "but this girl has been brought up like I don't know what. A nothing, a heathen. Did Hitler care whether anyone was half-Jewish? They all went into the gas chambers the same way!" She wiped the tears that were filling her eyes. "I'm not one to say I told you so, but I knew it, I knew it. . . ."

"Mama, please." Mrs. Barnes stretched out her hand to pat her mother. Her face was miserable. "This is a happy occasion. Let's not dig up the past. Peter and I have been married for nineteen years. Sophie's a grown girl. I suppose it's my fault that she doesn't know much about being Jewish." She looked at her mother pleadingly. "But now that we're back in town maybe you can help me. We can teach her together."

"How can you teach someone about being Jewish? It's in here," said Mrs. Golden, touching her breast. "It's in your heart that you have to feel it." She looked around at her brood, who had been keeping an uneasy, embarrassed silence. "I'm an old woman and maybe I don't know much, but one thing I'm sure of. If anyone of you at this table, except Peter, ever forgets for one minute that you're Jewish, it'll be a sad day. Not just for me, but for you too. Hitler may be dead, but his ideas aren't. And you too, Peter. You have to remember that you married a Jewish girl; you can't forget that."

"I don't want to forget it," Mr. Barnes said quietly. "But I married Esther because I love her, not because she's Jewish. Religion has not been an important part of our household."

"It's not up to me to tell you how to run your home," Mrs. Golden said. "I'm not asking you to keep a kosher house." She shrugged her shoulders. "You should excuse me, but you wouldn't understand. Being a Jew is more than a religion. It's not the same as just going to one church or another."

"Come, Sophie, don't look so sad. You did nothing wrong." Her grandfather was trying to change the conversation. "Come on, Dora, bring in the meat. Talk, talk, talk. No butter, but there's no meat either."

The conversation at the table started up again, and yet Sophie felt her stomach churning. She was upset by the obvious tensions that existed between her grandmother and her mother, and she did not want to become involved, but that concern was only part of what was bothering her. Things had been said, and looks exchanged, that worried her. She had a strong and unpleasant feeling that pressure was going to be put on her in a certain direction. Even the few things that Rachel had said were an indication. But, she said to herself, the fact remained that she *was* only half-Jewish, and no one could change that!

Sophie's fears were confirmed as she and her parents were leaving to go home. Grandma Dora hugged Sophie hard. "I'm glad you came to Woodview," Mrs. Golden said. "I'll make a good Jewish girl of you yet."

Sophie didn't answer. Riding home in the car, however, she expressed her thoughts aloud. "I'm not so sure I want to be 'a good Jewish girl.'"

"Let's not talk about it now," Mr. Barnes said, catching the stricken look on his wife's face. "We're happy the way you are, Sophie."

"I'm not so sure," Mrs. Barnes murmured. "I'm not so sure at all."

III

A few nights later Sophie heard her mother sobbing through the wall of their rooms. She could not remember her mother ever crying before, and the sound frightened her. Sophie was not an eavesdropper, but when her own name was mentioned by her father she could not resist. Quiet and tense, she sat up in her bed and listened.

"You mustn't let Sophie upset you so," Mr. Barnes said gently.

"I can't bear the way she mopes around looking so unhappy. I feel as if we've made a terrible mistake. Maybe my mother was right. Maybe we shouldn't have gotten married." Mrs. Barnes's voice was choked.

"That's a silly thing to say after all these years. Sophie's having a rough time leaving her school and moving up here. She'll get over it." Mr. Barnes was speaking softly, but Sophie could hear every word. "You're reading things into her behavior."

"I'm afraid not. Every time I ask her to come over to Mama's with me, she turns up her nose. I have this awful feeling that we've brought up a snob. I honestly think she hates the idea of being Jewish." Mrs. Barnes's sobs were subsiding, but her voice was unhappy.

"The whole idea is new to her. Suddenly she's faced with what amounts to a new Jewish family. But I don't want you to get sick about it. Sophie will be all right. If she doesn't want to be Jewish, it'll be no great loss," he added philosophically.

"How can you say such a thing about your own daughter? Don't you care how she thinks?" Her mother seemed outraged by her father's calm outlook.

"Yes, I care if she turns out to be a snob with ridiculous prejudices. But she'll have to find her own way. I don't know that I care terribly if she thinks of herself as Jewish or not. What does being Jewish mean to most of the Jews we know?"

"Sophie asked me that question once. What does being Jewish mean? You don't understand, because you're not. I guess it's a tribal feeling more than anything, a rather fierce sense of belonging to a people who've been pushed around for two thousand years. You either have it or you don't. How can I expect you to understand?" Mrs. Barnes asked helplessly.

"Esther, don't turn away from me." Her father's voice was hurt.

Sophie got up and walked away from the bed. She didn't want to hear any more. At the window she sank down on the floor and put her head on the windowsill. She felt terrible: guilty, confused, and alone. Very much alone. Those two had each other for comfort and understanding, but she had no one. She wondered if she were anti-Semitic, and if she were, was it such a crime? Did a person have to love everyone? Did a girl have to love everyone in her family?

Sophie stared out the window. She wished she could snoop out the story of her parents' marriage, really know what had gone on. Feeling guilty about her own thoughts, she wished they had been stopped. They never should have married, and now they had to take the consequences. The situation wasn't her fault.

She let resentment and anger replace her sense of guilt, clinging to the fact that what had happened nineteen years ago, before she was ever thought of, was not of her doing.

The opening of school was a great relief to Sophie. Her cousin Rachel had offered to pick her up and take her the first day, but Sophie had politely though firmly insisted that she preferred going by herself. She was determined not to be drawn into a clique before she had a chance to look around and choose her own friends. Coming to school under Rachel's auspices, even though Rachel was only a sophomore, would have made that difficult.

The high school was a modern, one-story, sprawling building on the outskirts of town, set back from the highway at the end of a long, attractive, tree-lined driveway. There was ample room for a ball field and athletic grounds. Sophie drove to school with her father the first day as the grade school was close by. "You'd better take the school bus home," Mr. Barnes told her, when he dropped her off. "I'll probably be late. Good luck," he added with a nod.

"Thank you." Sophie smiled at her father. She didn't feel nervous and was mildly surprised at her confidence. However, she knew there was nothing to be nervous about. This public high school in a small town could only be a comedown after the Beardsley School for Girls. Looking around at the other girls, Sophie felt that she was better dressed and probably better educated.

In her classroom, Sophie found herself, for the first time in her life, spotting the Jewish clique. She didn't know why she was sure they were Jewish—there weren't many of them, three girls and two boys—but she recognized them immediately. They weren't really different from the others, perhaps a little more stylishly dressed, a little more vivacious, yet there was a separateness about them and a communication among them that gave them a distinct mark. Her mother once had said that a Jew can recognize a Jew anywhere in the world, and Sophie wondered if this remark were true. The whole idea made her feel uncomfortable. Was she marked in the same way?

At lunchtime one of the Jewish girls came over to introduce herself. "You're Rachel Golden's cousin, aren't you? I'm Shirley Hertzberg. We'd love you to have lunch with us." She was a tall, slim, pretty girl with bright eyes and a warm smile.

Fully aware of her determination not to identify herself

with the Jewish crowd right away, Sophie still couldn't say no. She smiled weakly and accepted the invitation.

Down in the cafeteria there was a large table where apparently Shirley and her friends usually ate. Sophie noticed that the girls sat separated from the boys. Her cousin Rachel was at the table, and seats had been saved for Shirley and herself. Rachel introduced Sophie around to the eight or nine girls, all of whom had Jewish last names.

Shirley sat down next to Sophie and immediately started talking to her. "What do you think of Woodview? It must be awful coming here after living in New York."

Sophie glanced across at her cousin Rachel. "Rachel doesn't think so. She hates New York."

"I adore it," Shirley said eagerly. She was an outgoing girl with a sophisticated, knowing air.

"I love New York," Sophie said.

"I hope you won't hate it here. You'll have to join the Community Center. It's really for the families who belong to the temple, but I'm sure it'll be all right for you. I don't imagine your parents want to become members of the temple," she added with some embarrassment.

"I'm quite sure they don't," Sophie said. "And thank you very much, but I don't think I want to join the Community Center."

Shirley was astonished. "But there's nothing to do around here if you don't. Of course, you can come as a guest first and see how you like it. As a matter of fact there's going to be a dance next Saturday night. I'll get a date for you, and you come with me and Robie, my date."

Sophie hesitated. She glanced around the cafeteria, and for no reason her eyes met the eyes of a boy sitting by himself at a table studying. He had just looked up at the same moment that she did. They didn't smile at each other, and he went back to his studying. He was an unusually handsome boy with heavy blond hair, a tanned skin, and bright blue eyes. Somehow he had the look of a loner, strong-minded and interesting. The kind of boy, Sophie thought, whose cool a girl would want to break through.

The chance glance helped Sophie make up her mind. "Thanks a lot, but I'm afraid not. We haven't really settled in yet, and I have a lot to do." Sophie was aware of how feeble her excuse sounded.

"Yes, of course, if you're busy," Shirley said coolly. If you want to be standoffish, go ahead, her eyes said, and she turned away from Sophie and began talking to the other girls.

Sophie was relieved when lunch was over. She had

never been in a situation like this one before; she was uneasy and yet convinced that she was doing the right thing. Even Abbie had warned her before she left New York, "Don't get mixed up with the wrong crowd in the beginning. That can be death. Play it cool until you find out who's who." And Abbie hadn't had the slightest notion that the wrong crowd could be a Jewish crowd.

Shirley Hertzberg was what Sophie's mother would call a *macher*, a Yiddish word for a person who thought herself very important and liked to manage other people's lives. Sophie was bothered when her mother used these strange, Yiddish words, yet having heard them, she often found herself privately using them in her own mind— which bothered her even more. Before the day was over Sophie saw clearly that as Shirley went so did the rest of the Jewish girls. And Shirley was going to make no more friendly advances to Sophie Barnes.

Only Rachel, with a troubled face, sought her out. Sophie was in study hall when she felt a nudge and found Rachel sitting beside her. Rachel spoke in a whisper. "I wish you could come to the dance Saturday night. You'd meet everyone. I mean, you don't have all that settling to do, do you? As Shirley said, how long does it take to unpack a few suitcases?"

"News gets around fast, doesn't it?" Sophie murmured.

43

"You're very sweet, Rachel, but I'd rather not. I'm new and I don't want to rush things. Besides, I really don't like blind dates," Sophie added, wishing she had thought of that excuse in the first place.

But she still wasn't convincing. "Any date you have here will have to be kind of blind, won't it? I mean you wouldn't know any boy very well no matter what. And there aren't that many Jewish boys."

"But he doesn't have to be Jewish. Not for me he doesn't," Sophie said, making up her mind that she might as well state her position outright.

Rachel's thin face was more troubled. "Of course, that's up to you. But as I told you, the crowds don't mix. And besides . . ." her voice trailed off in embarrassment.

"You mean no Gentile boy is going to ask me out?" Sophie asked.

"Well, if you went out with a Gentile boy, everyone would think it was funny. They wouldn't like it," Rachel said, leaving who "they" was vague.

"I don't care what *they* think, whoever *they* are," Sophie said. "I don't believe in discrimination of any kind, and I think this business of worrying about whether someone is Gentile or Jewish is ridiculous. I don't intend to subscribe to it."

44

"It's different in a small town," Rachel said helplessly. There was a resigned look on her face. "I'm sorry."

The younger girl turned to her books. Sophie was tempted to put out her hand and say something that would be friendly, but her indignation got the best of her, and she too opened a book and silently started to study.

IV

Thinking about it afterward, Sophie often wondered how she ever survived that first week in school. Every afternoon she came home and went to her room and wept. Every person in the senior class seemed to belong to a group except herself, and no one, except Shirley Hertzberg, who had given up the first day, made any attempt to take her in. She never had hated any place so intensely in her life.

On Friday afternoon her mother came into her room. Sophie was stretched out on her bed, face down. She jumped up, startled by her mother's voice. "Aunt Sara told me that you said you couldn't go to a dance tomorrow night. She said they had a nice boy for you to go with. What's the matter with you, Sophie?"

Sophie shook her head wearily. "Nothing's the matter. I just don't feel like going to that dance. For heaven's sake, why is everyone making such a big deal of it?"

"No one's making a big deal." Mrs. Barnes was keeping her voice quiet. "But do you think I like to watch you come home every day and lie on your bed? You cry in the afternoon, and I cry at night. What for? You'd think some tragedy had happened. Your father found a good job that he likes, and we moved to a town where you have family and could have all the friends you want. And real friends —your own kind—not those society girls who would have dropped you the minute you graduated anyhow. Do you think you would have seen any of them after school was over? Or met any nice boys you might want to marry?"

Sophie was livid with rage. "You mean a nice Jewish boy! How can you talk to me this way? You didn't marry a nice Jewish boy. Why all of a sudden does everyone want me to be Jewish? You married a *goy*, not me. You should have thought of this when you married Father. Didn't it every occur to you that maybe you weren't going to produce a nice Jewish daughter?"

"I never thought I'd have a daughter who hated her people. Your father and I fell in love, and he accepted my Jewishness. We both always assumed our children would be Jewish, he as much as I." There were tears in her mother's eyes.

"I guess you assumed wrong. I don't hate any people —you can't accuse me of that. All I did was say I didn't want to go to a dance. Please leave me alone." Sophie put her face back on the pillow and waited until her mother left the room.

Never had she felt such terrible despair. She clung to the thought that if she hadn't left New York this dreadful abyss between two worlds would never have opened up. Yet she could not help admitting that sooner or later she would have had to face the same dilemma. But I wish it were later, she thought, this is the worst time in my whole life.

There was one tiny bright spot in her life at school, although as Sophie told herself it wasn't anything to get excited about. The boy whom she had seen the first day in the cafeteria was in most of her classes and sat next to her in English and Math. They had established a sort of rapport that was as much an exchange of glances as it was of words. He wasn't quite the loner he had seemed at first, although she couldn't figure out who his close friends were. He seemed friendly with everyone, and yet he kept to himself. Perhaps he has no close friends, Sophie thought, which made her feel that they might have something basic in common. She longed to know him better, but she couldn't get beyond the polite, friendly wall that surrounded him.

During the second week in school, however, Sophie made a friend. She was waiting for the school bus in the afternoon when a girl who was in her classes came over to her. "You're Rachel Golden's cousin, aren't you? I'm Patti Stuart. I live near you, and I have my car today. I thought maybe you'd like to ride home with me instead of waiting for the bus."

"That would be great," Sophie said warmly. "Thanks."

Patti was an attractive girl, who needed to lose around fifteen pounds to be stunning. She had a strong, beautifully molded face and head, good legs, and the height to carry her weight well, but she was too heavy.

"How do you like Woodview?" Patti asked the conventional question, once they were in her small sports car.

"Not much," Sophie told her. "But I don't know it well yet."

"You won't like it any better when you do," Patti said drily. "It's cliquey. You're either in or you're out, and each clique stays together."

"That's what I figured," Sophie said gloomily.

"There are a few exceptions. I'm one of them. I hate cliques. Besides I'm a Catholic, so I don't belong to the Youth Fellowship in the Episcopal Church or to the Community Center. The YF is a group of young people the minister organized. They have discussions and socials and things. I don't like these divisions. I have all kinds of friends, but no one real close."

"I feel the same way you do," Sophie said eagerly. The more Patti talked, the more she liked her. "Who's that blond boy who sits next to me in English? I think his name is Ricky Taylor. He doesn't seem to belong to any one bunch either."

Patti had stopped the car in front of Sophie's house, but the two girls stayed in it talking. "Ricky's an oddball. I don't really know him. He comes from a snooty family, but I don't think he's the way they are. His mother's an awful pill. She looks down her nose at everyone—no one's good enough for Mrs. Taylor. The only reason he's not away at some fancy prep school is because his mother's president of the school board and people would have a fit if she sent her son to a private school. I don't know who he's dating now, if he is. You interested?" She asked the question with a wide smile.

"I think he's attractive," Sophie said. "And he's been friendly, that's all."

"I wouldn't count on him." Patti looked as if she wanted to say something more, but hesitated.

"What's the matter? Say it," Sophie said.

"Well, I don't think Rick would date a Jewish girl. I don't think it would matter to him," Patti added quickly, "but it would to his family."

Sophie could feel her resentment rising. "I never heard of people anywhere in the world so conscious of race and religion as the people in this town! It's terrible. We never gave any of this a thought in New York!"

Patti asked Sophie what kind of a school she had gone to and if she'd done much dating. "In a girls' school it would be different," Patti said wisely. "And in an elementary school no one cares. But when teen-agers start to date, then everyone worries about them going steady and later getting married. That's the heart of the trouble."

"But my parents intermarried, and it worked for them," Sophie said indignantly.

"Did it? It may have worked for them, but what about you? I notice you're not so chummy with the Jewish girls, and the others aren't so chummy with you."

51

"I haven't been here very long," Sophie spoke defensively, but her face was troubled. "I've talked more to you than I have to anyone." She turned to Patti gratefully. "I hope you and I can be friends."

"Of course we can," Patti said warmly. "I'm a little bit in the same boat that you are. I don't mix too well myself."

"Misery loves company," Sophie said with a wry smile. "Thanks a million for the ride—and for everything."

Mrs. Barnes appeared relieved to see that her daughter at last came home from school with a smile on her face, but she was sensible enough not to ask questions.

With Patti to encourage her, Sophie made up her mind to try to break through Ricky Taylor's reserve. "What have you got to lose?" Patti asked. "I may be dead wrong about him. He may hate his parents."

Sophie dressed with more care for school and continued to disassociate herself from the clique made up of Shirley Hertzberg and Rachel Golden and their friends. As Patti pointed out, it was the only one she could have joined anyway. "Up here," Patti said, "the name Barnes doesn't mean a thing. You're Rachel's cousin, and everyone thinks of you as another one of the Golden girls whether you like it or not. The Golden family is well known, and you're part of it."

Finally one day in the cafeteria, when Sophie came down late for lunch, she saw Ricky sitting by himself as he often did. The cafeteria was filled, and there was no empty table. Sophie screwed up her courage and went over to him. "Do you mind if I sit here?" she asked.

"No, not at all." He jumped up and stood until she sat down. At least, his mother taught him some manners, Sophie noticed with satisfaction, although his formality made her shy. However, when out of the corner of her eye she saw Shirley at a nearby table lean over and whisper something that she knew was about herself, she was more determined than ever to make friends with Ricky.

She found him easy to talk to, in a cool, remote fashion that she rather liked. He had decided opinions, and she began making a mental list of the many things he hated: ketchup on his hamburger, the color pink (worn by a girl), the noise in the cafeteria, meaningless chatter, most of his teachers, life in Woodview.

"Do you like anything?" Sophie asked. "A psychologist would say that you are filled with hostility."

"I like a lot of things, but I'm filled with hostility too. Isn't everyone?" he asked with a charming smile.

"What do you like?" Sophie asked.

"I like music, records. I like quiet, I like books, I like girls—some girls—I like woods, except most of them around here are gone. I like to sleep. I could sleep for days on end if they'd let me. I like movies too. How's that for a list?"

"Pretty good. Except it doesn't say much for people. Most everything you like one does alone. You're not very social."

"You're right, I'm not. I'm not social at all. Is that bad?" Ricky's eyes were humorous.

"It's not good. I'm afraid of anti-social people. They're destructive." Sophie smiled back at him.

"I'm an innocent anti-social person. I don't do anything except mind my own business."

"I have no quarrel with that," Sophie said quietly.

Ricky laughed. "Just when I thought I was building up to a good argument you let me down. We'll continue later," he said, when the bell rang for classes to start.

Sophie treasured his last words. They meant that he was going to make some move to talk to her again. She had made a good start, the initiative was up to him now, and she had to sit tight and wait.

Waiting was the hardest thing in the world. She wondered what he would do. Would he telephone her at home? Would he know how to get her number? Would he suggest that they have lunch together again? Her speculation led her in all directions, and at home each time the telephone rang she jumped.

Ricky took his time about picking up their friendship. In their classes he was affable as he always had been, but he withdrew again into his shell. He was like a hazelnut that she wanted to crack open so she could enjoy the sweet meat inside. His slightly sulky, arrogant look was provocative and exciting, driving her into wild schemes of ways to demand his attention. She went so far as to consider fainting in front of him or falling down, frantic in her desire to put on a dramatic act to break through his aloofness.

Her opportunity to make a further contact with him came from the most unexpected source. One morning at breakfast her father said that he had to go to a meeting of the school board at Mrs. Taylor's house, although he had arranged to leave his car at the garage to have it serviced. He could get a ride over to Mrs. Taylor's, but asked Sophie to pick up his car and come and get him around five o'clock. Sophie agreed with alacrity.

This opening was perfect. Naturally she had to ask Ricky for directions to get to his house and to tell him why she wanted them. He seemed amused by the coincidence and suggested that she come over earlier. In a flutter of excitement, Sophie went home after school to fool with her hair, to change her clothes, to loll in front of the mirror trying different effects with and without makeup.

Sophie's aunts were at the house with her mother, and she could hear her name mentioned downstairs, but she couldn't make out what they were saying. Undoubtedly they were repeating the same old stuff: why wasn't she mixing with the Jewish girls, why was she such a snob, why was she breaking her mother's heart and her grandmother's too?

Sophie resented her own wave of remorse. Her sense of guilt was emotional and unfounded, she reasoned. Her point of view was as valid as theirs. She thought that the Jewish girls and boys were the snobs; they were the ones who preferred to stick by themselves and not mix with the others. They had no right to call anyone anti-Semitic when they were the ones who segregated themselves. In a way she was lucky, because she was neither one thing nor the other and should be free to mix easily with any group.

She brushed her long hair until it shone like a satin cap on her head and decided on no makeup. Once again she examined her tanned face and long, slim body in the mirror. No one could say that she looked Jewish, and the delight that this observation gave her was a secret she would keep to herself.

Sophie drove the car slowly out to the Taylor house. She didn't want to arrive too early. The unfamiliar, pretty road led her out of town and wound past the church Ricky had mentioned, the red barn on the left, the sharp curve in the road, and there were the stone posts marking the entrance to Clatter Valley Farm.

Of course, as Ricky had said, their place wasn't a farm anymore, but everyone knew it as such so they had kept the name.

It was anything but a farm, Sophie thought, as she drove through the driveway between the stone walls. It was a beautiful estate with rolling lawns and tall trees, a tennis court and swimming pool, and an imposing house. Tall columns guarded the front entrance and sprawling wings stretched out on either side. Sophie was afraid of the house; she could never be at ease with Ricky there, and she wished she hadn't come. Her entire home would fit into one wing of this place.

But it was too late now to turn back. She stopped the car where the other cars were parked, near a side porch and entrance. Not knowing whether to go in there or to walk around to the front of the house, she decided on the latter and gathered up her courage to use the large, shiny brass knocker. A maid in a neat uniform answered the door promptly, but before Sophie had a chance to say anything Ricky appeared.

He gave her a warm welcome and suggested that they wait outside until the meeting was over. He took her around the grounds to show her the gardens, still in bloom with autumn flowers in September, the tennis court, and the pool. "It's so beautiful. You must love it," Sophie said. They were sitting in a screened summerhouse that had a lovely view across a stream and into the hills beyond.

"I do. I love this place. That's one of the contradictions. I love it too much." Looking at his face now, Sophie realized that sulkiness was not what characterized Ricky's face, but anger. He turned an angry face to the world, looking as if he wanted to smash his fists against an enemy. But who was the enemy whom he hated so intensely?

"I don't know what you mean," Sophie said.

"The place is beautiful, but it represents something rotten. The big manor house with lots of servants. The whole life is so seductive that I'm afraid of it. Ordering people around can get to be a habit. The next thing you start to think that you're superior."

"Do you think you're superior?" Sophie asked.

Ricky laughed. "Certainly not. Listen, I've been wanting to ask you out, but I've been scared to. My mother would have a fit if I dated you, and I wouldn't be surprised if your family felt the same. You understand?"

Sophie was astonished by his frankness. Her first reaction was one of resentment. She felt that he was treating her as an object, not as a person. "I really am not interested in your inner struggles," she said coldly.

"Oh, nuts. I've made a mess of this. I was only trying to be honest. Will you go out with me?"

His face was open, and she was convinced of his sincerity. "Of course, I'll go out with you," Sophie said with a little laugh. "I won't hold your background against you."

"It's a date. Saturday night. I'll pick you up after dinner. Okay?"

"Okay."

Sophie saw her father come out of the house so she and Ricky walked back to meet him.

Mr. Barnes was waiting in the car for Sophie. One look at his face told her that he was in a bad temper. His usually placid face was both angry and troubled.

"Is everything all right?" Sophie asked, as they drove away.

"That woman is impossible. She's stupid and bigoted. She's fighting against everything I want to do for the school. 'Why do we need remedial reading?' she asks. 'Can't we teach the children how to read? What do these children need French for? They'll never use it!' She is the worst snob. . . . I didn't know people like her existed. And, to top it all, she keeps calling me Mr. Golden, because I came here under the auspices of the Goldens. What an awful anti-Semite." Sophie had never seen her father so angry.

Sophie kept silent. This was no time to tell her father that she was going out with Ricky Taylor.

V

It was Friday evening. Shabbas, her grandfather called it, meaning the Sabbath. Silently Sophie watched her grandmother put a shawl over her head and light the tall, slim candles held in the silver candlesticks. Mrs. Golden's lips moved rapidly in a low Hebrew prayer ushering in the Sabbath that started with Friday at sundown and ended with Saturday at the same time.

Sophie could not follow or understand the many contradictions in her grandparents' household. Why did her grandmother light candles with a prayer every Friday night but at the same time have no compunction about riding in a car or turning on an electric light, which, it was explained to Sophie, Orthodox Jews did not do on Shabbas? Why did her grandmother never serve butter or dairy dishes with meat, according to the kosher law, but sometimes go to a restaurant for lobster, which was forbidden?

At the dinner table that night, when the family was gathered for the traditional Friday night meal, everyone tried to give answers to Sophie. Grandpa Golden said a prayer over the freshly baked *challah*, and while they ate the soup with matzoh balls, the *gefilte* fish, the roast chicken and carrots, the dessert of home-baked *schnecken*, and drank the tea or coffee, they all talked. Grandma, who looked young and dashing to be the head of such a brood, was flustered by Sophie's questions. "As if you could learn about being Jewish from a book," she said with exasperation.

She interrupted regularly to alternate between chiding her daughter for bringing up a Gentile and defending her position. "Suddenly for her, I'm not a good enough Jew," she said bristling. "I do what I feel is right. I like to light the candles. I used to watch my mother light them every

Friday. But not to ride in a car today or to turn on an electric light—that seems foolish to me. In the old days it was hard work to make a fire or go somewhere, and everyone was supposed to rest and pray on the Sabbath, but today it's no work, and we don't pray so much. Jews keep up with the times, like everybody else."

Uncle Harry explained that many Orthodox Jews still obeyed the old laws, but that the Reform Jews had adapted them to modern times. "The Jews have to be adaptable," Uncle Harry said. "They've had to live in so many different countries that they've developed a practical flexibility in order to keep alive."

The aunts spoke of the culture of the Jews, their special kind of humor, the wisdom of the old Talmudic scholars, and, even though there was an introspective, melancholy strain in many Jews, their strong reaffirmation for life. "Otherwise they wouldn't have survived all these centuries," Aunt Sara said.

Nevertheless, Sophie was still confused. What made people Jews, and why did they want to remain Jews if they had so much trouble? She kept asking herself these questions, but she could not find the answers for them.

Rachel was cool to Sophie that evening. Her dark glances made Sophie feel uncomfortable, as if Rachel knew things that she didn't know and that boded no good.

A few times Sophie was tempted to take Rachel aside and ask her directly what the trouble was, but she suspected what the answer would be, and she didn't want to hear it. Sophie decided that if she were to be ostracized for not wanting to join a Jewish clique, the problem would be theirs, not hers. They were the ones being exclusive and snobbish.

After dinner, Aunt Helen sat down at the piano and played old songs. The family gathered around and sang hits from ancient musical comedies, each one eager for his favorite. Grandma grew nostalgic about the twenties, when she was a flapper, and tried, not too successfully, to show Rachel and Sophie what the Charleston was like. Everyone was very jolly, and Grandpa brought out a bottle of sweet wine, which he called schnapps, although his sons said he was fooling them because schnapps was usually stronger stuff.

Sophie kept watching her father, impressed by the way he fitted in and seemed at home, although every once in a while someone made a joke about his being a *goy*. Mr. Barnes took the remarks good-naturedly, although Sophie could not help but wonder if the banter did not hide the deeper resentments that had arisen when her mother had first announced that she was marrying a Gentile. Sophie's parents had met while her father was at the university in

Worcester, and her mother, who had not gone to college, was taking extension courses and working in the university office. Slowly Sophie was beginning to see what her mother must have gone through to buck her family, and she marveled at her courage. But she still resented her mother's desire for her to be Jewish. Was her mother sorry now for what she had done? Was she feeling guilty about it? Or did it all come from Grandma Dora?

Saturday morning Sophie knew that she had to tell her parents that she was going out with Ricky Taylor that night. She also knew that they weren't going to like the date, and the more she thought about it the angrier she became.

She made her announcement at the breakfast table, carefully waiting until her parents had had their first cup of coffee. "I have a date tonight," she said, as casually as she could.

Her mother beamed. "That's nice. Who are you going out with? I bet it's that nice Kahn boy. He's so attractive looking."

"No, it's not the Kahn boy," Sophie said flatly. "I'm going out with Ricky Taylor."

Her mother didn't know who Ricky Taylor was, but her father did immediately. And he exploded. "Of all the kids in this whole town, you certainly picked out the worst one. His family is known to be the most bigoted, the most anti-Semitic. I told you what his mother is like. She is a mean woman, plain and simple."

"That Taylor family. I know who they are," Mrs. Barnes said. "I forgot they had a son your age. You can't go out with him, Sophie."

"What do you mean, I can't go out with him? I can't believe you two. You simply don't make sense. First of all, I think I'm old enough to choose my own friends, and I'm not going out with Ricky's mother. I'm going out with him, and he happens to be a very nice boy, who is not anti-Semitic at all. He knows who I am and he asked me for the date; I didn't ask him. But, besides, how can you two sit there and tell me I can't go out with a Gentile boy?" Sophie's anger made her blue eyes shine and her face crimson.

"No one said you can't go out with a Gentile boy," Mrs. Barnes said. "But you can't go out with someone from that anti-Semitic family."

"Well, Ricky isn't anti-Semitic, and I'm going out with him," Sophie said vehemently.

"The anti-Semitism is beside the point," Mr. Barnes said. "By this time everyone knows that Mrs. Taylor is out to see that I don't get tenure at the end of the year. She's been gunning for me from the first day that I arrived. It seems to me you could find someone else to date besides her son."

"I'm sorry, Dad, but for tonight I can't. I happen to like Ricky, and I'm going out with him. I can't be responsible for what his mother does, and I don't think he can. For people who profess to be liberals, you two are acting like people out of the dark ages."

"We're not asking you to be responsible for Mrs. Taylor," Mr. Barnes said wearily. "We're asking you for some understanding of our position."

"All I can say is that I'm sorry that you feel the way you do, but you have to understand my position, too."

Sophie left the dining room and went upstairs to her room. She never used to battle with her parents this way before, but ever since they had left New York there seemed to be one fight after another.

Sophie was in a turmoil about her evening's date. She spent the afternoon fussing with her hair—pinning it up, leaving it down—and going through her closet trying on clothes. Running through her excitement, however, was a nagging worry about her parents. Naturally she had done things in her life that her parents didn't approve of— mostly things they didn't know about like smoking cigarettes in Abbie's bathroom—but never before had she clashed openly with them and consciously decided to go her own way. A turning point in her life had come. She was a separate entity, a human being in her own right, who had to make her own valuations and judgments. Previously she had relied on her parents for important decisions; even when she had argued with them she almost always had ended up doing what they thought best. Now she was disregarding their wishes entirely. The thought that she was stepping out on her own was scary, yet she was convinced that she was right in choosing her own friends and in rejecting her parents' old-fashioned sectarianism.

Sophie made a point of being ready when Ricky arrived to pick her up, as she didn't want to leave him with her parents. She was downstairs and waiting so that he came into the house for only a moment. After hasty introductions to her mother and father, they left.

"Where to?" Ricky asked, as he drove away.

"That's up to you. This is your beat, not mine," Sophie told him.

Ricky drove his sports car expertly, and Sophie's spirits picked up when he drove out of Woodview. He looked very handsome in his blue shirt, striped tie, and navy blazer. His tall, blond good looks were so . . . well, so *American*, Sophie thought. In her secret heart she had hoped living in Woodview might mean riding through the night in an open car with her hair flying (she finally had left it down) and a handsome boy at the wheel. She had been waiting to write to Abbie until she had something to say, and this date was it! Ricky was the most attractive boy in Woodview, and she had picked him out. His clothes were well cut, casual, and he had an air of self-confidence. In spite of his hostilities and his cynicism toward his parents, Ricky had the assurance of a person not only endowed with good looks but armed with the knowledge that he came from a privileged segment of society.

Ricky drove on into Worcester. There he parked the car, and they walked down Main Street looking for a movie. They talked about Woodview and about school, and Sophie felt that he was in many ways as much alone as she. She had glimpses of a life that like her own had been shielded and protected and lonely, and that now many of the values he had been brought up to regard as true and right had become suspect to him. To discover that someone who, on the surface, seemed to have everything— looks, money, social position—was as dissatisfied and confused as she was both comforting and disturbing. She was especially surprised a boy would feel this way. Like most girls, Sophie had always believed that life was much easier for a boy, and they were relatively free of inner conflicts and problems.

"I used to want to be a boy when I was young," Sophie confided to Ricky. "But I've changed my mind about that."

"Well, being a boy isn't all that great. A boy may have more freedom, but he also has more things to worry about. No one's ever going to take care of him; he has to look out for himself. And then there's the draft, and learning about how he feels about killing people. I don't understand how a guy who wouldn't shoot a woodchuck in his backyard can be trained to take a gun and shoot people, to drop bombs that are going to kill women and children. Why do they do it? Is it patriotism? Is it fear? What's behind it?"

"Thank goodness, I'll never have to make a decision like that," Sophie said. "I have all I can do choosing a shampoo when I go to the store, let alone having to decide if I'm willing to go to war or not."

They soon found a movie that they both wanted to see. In the theater Sophie kept strictly in the center of her seat, careful not to lounge toward Ricky, until his hand reached over and picked up one of hers. She looked around, they smiled at each other in the darkness, and Sophie relaxed close beside him.

After the movie Ricky suggested that they go to what he described as the only "nearly swinging" place in Worcester. It was a teen-age hangout where a combo played on Saturday nights. Ricky took her away from Main Street, and she followed him down a few steps into what had probably once been a downstairs apartment or basement. Now it was teeming with young people sitting at booths and tables. A tiny place was cleared for dancing, and up on a platform four boys were playing music with abandon. It was quite dark, the noise was deafening, and there didn't seem to be room for any more people, but Ricky found a table. He ordered ginger ale and sandwiches, and they danced. Whatever shyness they each may have felt quickly disappeared under the influence of the fast music. They were both good dancers, and the dance floor was one place where they could lose their inhibitions and let themselves go.

The time flew by and the place was thinning out when a whole new crowd came in. Sophie looked up from her table and saw Shirley Hertzberg and her cousin Rachel in the group of boys and girls. Immediately she knew that they had come from the usual Saturday night dance at the Community Center. All of them stared at her, but only Rachel came over to say hello, and she came with some embarrassment. Although she was cordial and pleasant, her forced gaiety revealed the effort she was making.

"I guess your friends don't think much of your going out with me," Ricky said, after Rachel had left them. "I've been wondering—and I hope you don't mind my asking—but are they boycotting you or you them?" he asked.

"It's mutual," Sophie said. "I've never been in a clique before, and I see no reason to start just because I've moved to a small town. I'm willing to be friends with everyone, but so far only you and Patti have shown any interest. They"—indicating the Jewish crowd who had put together a group of small tables for themselves—"complain about discrimination, but they're the ones who want to stick together."

"That's what my mother says," Ricky told her. "She says the Jewish people are much happier by themselves, so why should people try to mix?"

Sophie nodded her head, yet she felt distinctly uncomfortable to find herself in agreement with Mrs. Taylor. That she, Sophie Barnes, and Mrs. Taylor, who was known to be anti-Semitic, should be on the same side of any argument seemed impossible.

Sophie couldn't bear the presence of Shirley and her friends, who either ignored Sophie and Ricky or gave them curious glances—"As if we had two heads!" Sophie exclaimed—and she and Ricky soon left. They were both quiet on the ride back to Woodview.

"I hope you're not sorry you went out with me," Ricky said, when they were almost home.

"I was thinking the same thing," Sophie said. "I'm certainly not sorry, and I hope you're not."

"Me? Of course not. I'm not out to prove anything. I asked you out because I like you." He stopped in front of her house.

"Thank you." Impulsively Sophie leaned over and kissed him on the cheek. "You were sweet to say that." She started to get out of the car, but Ricky held her back. "Don't tease," he said, and kissed her firmly on the mouth. "Good night, Soph, see you Monday," he said.

She watched him drive off, and before he turned the corner he waved. The house was dark, except for a light in the hall, and Sophie tiptoed upstairs so as not to awaken her parents.

She felt excited and stimulated by the evening, and she

didn't want to answer questions or face disapproval. She preferred to be alone, not to think, but to enjoy her own feelings. She liked Ricky very much and took satisfaction in striking out for herself.

VI

Sophie's dates with Ricky became a regular Saturday night pattern, yet the shadow of their parents' disapproval hung over their relationship. Sophie knew that Mr. and Mrs. Taylor didn't welcome the fact of his taking her out any more than her parents did. Ricky rarely talked about the situation, and she sensed that he didn't want to come right out and say that his parents didn't like her, but little things slipped out, and happened, that made their feelings clear.

Sophie was able to talk with Patti much more openly than with Ricky. The two girls saw each other constantly and stayed overnight with each other often so that they could stay up late talking. Sophie refused to admit that Mr. and Mrs. Taylor didn't approve of her because she was Jewish. "First of all, I'm only half-Jewish," she argued with Patti, "and besides it's ridiculous. This is America. People don't care about that."

Patti laughed. "Don't be silly. A lot of people don't even like Catholics. Mrs. Taylor is a terrible anti-Semite, believe me."

"I think she's just a possessive mother. Ricky's an only child, and I'll bet she wouldn't like any girl he took out."

Patti's face was guarded. "I don't know. Ricky's dated girls before—girls whose parents belong to their Country Club and go to the right church—and Mrs. Taylor has been all lovey-dovey. She's given dinner dances at the club, and the Taylors have taken Ricky and his date into Boston to the theater and things like that. Have you ever been invited to his house?"

Sophie shook her head. "I went once to pick up my father, but that wasn't an invitation. Still a boy doesn't always invite a girl to his house. Anyway I don't care what

Mrs. Taylor thinks. I'm not going out with her. People around here are too suspicious. I never saw anything like it."

"Of course you didn't," Patti said, laughing. "You never lived in a small town before. On the surface everything seems lovely, and underneath there are all kinds of prejudices. Your grandfather, Mr. Golden, is a very respected man in town, but let him try to join the Country Club, or encourage the older teen-agers to mingle, or try to get on the school board, and you'll see what happens. You're very naïve."

"I don't agree," Sophie said. "I think my grandfather hasn't tried any of these things, because he's scared to, not because someone would stop him. Don't you believe that we have a democracy in this country?" Sophie demanded.

"There are a lot of Negroes who don't think so," Patti retorted. "I've been living in Woodview a long time, and I know what it's like."

A few weeks after this conversation Sophie came home and noticed on the hall table a flyer that was a reminder of a Board of Education meeting. Like most of their meetings, except executive sessions, it was public, and because the school curriculum was to be discussed the P.T.A. was seeking a good attendance.

At the dinner table that night Mr. Barnes was tense and

jittery. "If that woman tries to beat me down tonight, I'm going to let her have it," he said. His usual amiable manner was belligerent. Sophie knew he was talking about Mrs. Taylor and her own heart started pounding. She couldn't stand the conflicts and antagonisms; why couldn't people accept each other as individuals and not as members of a group?

"I'm going to the meeting. Are you coming?" Mrs. Barnes asked Sophie.

"No, why should I?" Sophie asked in surprise.

"It's rather an important meeting for your father, and I thought it would be a good idea if you came," her mother said.

"I really don't see why," Sophie said.

"It would do you good to see your boy friend's mother in action," Mrs. Barnes said grimly. "I'd like you to come."

Sophie shrugged. "If you insist, I will. But I'll tell you right now that nothing Mrs. Taylor does will affect how I feel about Ricky."

"I can see you have an open mind." Mr. Barnes spoke with a humorless smile.

"Just as much as you have," Sophie retorted sharply.

The school auditorium was well filled when Sophie arrived with her parents. Her father joined the members of the Board of Education at a table facing the auditorium. She and her mother sat with her aunts and uncles and grandparents, all of whom had come to the meeting. A certain amount of business was disposed of before the board opened up the discussion among themselves on the matter of elementary curriculum. Later the visitors would be given an opportunity to speak.

Mr. Barnes was asked first to give his report and recommendations. Sophie was proud of her father when he stood up to speak. He showed no sign of his earlier tenseness, his lean, sensitive face was relaxed, and he spoke vigorously and clearly. Without downgrading the educational program of the school system, he pointed out that the reading level of the students was below standard, and that both gifted students and slow students were not receiving sufficient attention. He had several recommendations: a part-time teacher for remedial reading, additional field trips, the introduction of a foreign language into the curriculum, and discussion of the possibility of certain honors programs and departmentalizing of classes from the fifth grade on. If the latter plan were adopted, the children would move from a homeroom teacher to a math class, English class, and so on.

Sophie watched Mrs. Taylor while her father was speaking. She was a tall, imposing, gray-haired woman with a tight, small mouth and heavy bags under her eyes. She had a milky white complexion, which she obviously nurtured and protected carefully from the ravages of sun or wind. Her face flushed, however, while Mr. Barnes was speaking, and she could barely control her impatience to speak until he finished.

The minute he sat down, she attacked everything he said with ill-concealed hostility. She defended the curriculum as it now stood and made cutting remarks about a newcomer wanting to change it and introducing what she called extravagant furbelows. She insinuated that what the children were getting was good enough for their needs and ended up with a meaningful look at the Golden family and a statement to the effect that "some people don't care how they throw around the taxpayers' money."

"She means the Jews," Aunt Sara whispered.

There was a hushed silence after Mrs. Taylor spoke, but then other members of the board spoke for Mr. Barnes's recommendations. The discussion went back and forth, with some of the board people arguing for the principal's position and one member, a Mr. Stacey, strongly supporting Mrs. Taylor. Before the meeting was turned over to a discussion among the visitors, it was announced that one of the school-board members was resigning because he was moving away. A successor would have to be chosen in a special election. The departing member supported Mr. Barnes, and Sophie could see the disappointment on her father's face.

In the discussion among the audience, made up mainly of parents, a majority were for Mr. Barnes's report, while some people argued for Mrs. Taylor's point of view. There was no question where the Goldens, the Hertzbergs, and the other Jewish families stood; they were firmly behind Mr. Barnes, but they were not alone.

Sophie had been shocked by the vehemence of Mrs. Taylor's attack. "But she had no reason," Sophie said in astonishment. "She was so patronizing, as if the children here didn't deserve the best education! She can't get away with that kind of attitude."

"She's been getting away with it for a number of years," Harry Golden said tartly. "She's the president of the board, and she carries a lot of weight. People think she keeps taxes down."

"We've told you how reactionary and prejudiced she is," Mrs. Barnes said reproachfully to Sophie.

On the way home in the car Mr. Barnes was dejected. "I never should have come up here. If I had known about that woman I wouldn't have accepted the job."

"You wouldn't have wanted to go someplace where nothing needed to be done, would you?" his wife said to him. "This is a real challenge. A lot of people don't agree with Mrs. Taylor. I think you can accomplish a great deal here. And I have some good news. Some of the audience were talking tonight about running Harry for the vacant position on the school board."

"Harry Golden?" Mr. Barnes was incredulous. "He doesn't stand a chance. Mrs. Taylor and Stacey will fight him tooth and nail. The town will never elect a Jew to the school board while she's president."

"Well, we'll see."

While they were talking Sophie was trying to sort out her own feelings. She was very disturbed by Mrs. Taylor's attitude; the woman's patronizing hostility made her feel resentful. She wanted to run away and fight back at the same time. Never had she reacted this way to anything before, as if she had fallen into a mud puddle in front of strangers and was furious and disgusted by their laughter. She tried to shrug off her emotions by classifying Mrs. Taylor as a stupid woman, yet she was neither stupid nor ignorant, and her insistent voice kept ringing in Sophie's ears. The one thing that she was clear about was her determination not to let her dislike for Mrs. Taylor confuse or enter into her friendship with Ricky.

The evening's experience gave her a stronger feeling

of tenderness for Ricky; how awful having such a mother must be for him!

That evening of the board meeting was the beginning of what soon became labeled by the people of Woodview as "the big mess," although there were many divergent interpretations of what was going on. "We always lived together here nicely," was a frequently repeated phrase, but it was usually followed by the comment that "it's been there smoldering all the time, something had to bring it to a head." No one gave a name to what "it" was, yet no one seemed the least doubtful about what "it" referred to.

Harry Golden was nominated to run for a seat on the Board of Education, and his campaign became a public, recognizable contest. But the choice between Harry Golden and Wilfred Parker, a close friend of Mrs. Taylor and Mr. Stacey, was not a simple, ordinary one. Harry Golden represented the Jewish community—although he was a grown man with a teen-age daughter of his own, he was still called Sam Golden's son—and Wilfred Parker was identified with the Country Club and the bank, where he worked with Mr. Taylor. The rest of the towns-people were divided up, those in favor of the educational innovations backing Harry Golden, those opposed supporting Mr. Parker, and many undecided. Political party affiliations temporarily lost their importance; whether one was a Democrat or a Republican didn't matter. Either a voter was going to show Mrs. Taylor that she couldn't run the town, or he was going to keep that Golden boy in his place because as Mrs. Taylor was reported to have remarked early in the campaign, "everyone knows that Jews don't care how much money they spend on education."

Later, when questioned in an interview, she did not deny the comment. This stand opened up a flood of letters in the newspapers, editorials, protests from the Jewish organizations and from the rabbi of the temple in Worcester. It also paved the way for a great many people, who accepted her statement as an uncritical but truthful evaluation, to come to Mrs. Taylor's defense. Charges of anti-Semitism were made, and the town was split wide open, leaving most people confused and wondering why the controversy had occurred in Woodview.

As Mr. Barnes said, "No one likes to admit that anti-Semitism exists. I must confess it is a revelation to me. The townspeople point to the Jewish families and say they live in nice houses, they have good businesses, what are they complaining about? Yet the Country Club is restricted, there are two developments on the lake that turned into clubs to keep Jews and Negroes out, and there are no Jews in the bank, on the hospital or library boards, or for that matter the Grange or the Volunteer Firemen. Everyone has been sweeping these prejudices under the rug."

Sophie felt that of all the people in town her personal life was hit the hardest by the clash. For everybody else it was a topic of conversation—except perhaps for her Uncle Harry, although she didn't think his life would be seriously affected by whether or not he got on the school board. But for her it meant that she must try to understand how she felt about who and what she was, and how she felt about Ricky. The last was her most pressing problem as her relationship with him seemed to be deepening all the time.

She saw Ricky as much as she could, and each time that she went out with him the pained expression on her mother's face appeared. Neither Sophie nor her parents talked about Ricky anymore, but the tension was always there.

The Wednesday before Thanksgiving the high school was dismissed at noon, and Sophie and Ricky decided to go away someplace for the afternoon and dinner. Ricky had his car, and he headed out into the country. "I feel like smelling some ocean air. Would you like a walk on a beach?" Ricky asked.

"Sounds good to me." It was one of those November days that was pleasant when the sun was out, but cold and wintry when the sun went behind the clouds.

Sophie relaxed on the seat beside Ricky. They spoke little on the ride out. Sophie sometimes thought that because they both left houses filled with so much tension they had to get used to one another anew each time they met. A period of adjustment was needed to re-establish their intimacy; sometimes they filled it with inconsequential chitchat, and often with a silence that Sophie felt they used to shed their at-home defenses.

Ricky drove her to a beach at the shore. It was a wonderful place with a long stretch of sand and a jetty of rock stretching out into the water. The beach was deserted on this windy November afternoon, but the huge, old-fashioned, Victorian seaside hotel facing the ocean was still impressive. Sophie could imagine ladies in white dresses sipping iced tea on the wide veranda and sedate couples playing croquet on the lawns under the trees.

Ricky and Sophie left their shoes and socks in the car and walked barefoot in the sand. They strolled as far as they could go in either direction, and then went out on the jetty and sat on the rocks. Neither one of them had mentioned the unmentionable—the public feud between their families—but it was in both their minds.

"It's so quiet and peaceful here," Sophie said, looking out over the water. The wind was sharp, but the sun had come out again and the warmth felt good on her bare legs.

"Yes." Ricky was lost in his own thoughts. Then suddenly he said, "I think you should join the Youth Fellowship group."

Sophie was startled. "What made you think of that now?"

"I've been thinking about it," Ricky said. "I think we're isolating ourselves, the two of us. I belong, but I haven't been going since you and I have been going together. And it's stupid to avoid it."

"What makes you think they'd let me join?" Sophie answered.

"There'd be no problem," Ricky said.

Sophie looked at him questioningly. "All right," he said. "If I sponsor you, you'll get in. What's so bad about that?" he asked defensively.

"I don't know." Sophie was dubious. "I don't know if I want to join. I'd have to think about it."

"It makes sense." Ricky's voice was persuasive. "You say you're not any one thing, being half and half, and this is a good way to prove it. It's a social group, not really religious, just some discussions sometimes. Why shouldn't you join? You'd be showing that Jews don't have to make their own ghetto."

"You're contradicting yourself," Sophie said. "First you say I should join because I'm not anything, and then you say I should join because I'm Jewish. Which is it?"

"It's both," Ricky said. "You'll prove one thing to yourself and another to the people who think of you as being Jewish."

"You certainly have it figured out." Sophie looked at him with wonder. She was proud of him, sitting there on the rocks with his hair mussed up, and she wished she could show him off to Abbie and her other friends in New York. They would say leave it to Sophie to pick the best-looking boy in all of Woodview and Worcester together. "Maybe I'll join. Maybe it's a good idea."

They sat talking and sunning themselves until the sun went down and it turned cold. Then they raced back to the car to get their shoes and coats. Ricky noticed that a few cars had appeared at the hotel. "I guess people come up for the Thanksgiving weekend," he said. "Want to have dinner here?"

"It looks as if it might be too elegant," Sophie said, looking down at her sweater and skirt. "I'm not dressed for a fancy hotel."

"It's not fancy. It doesn't get that kind of a crowd. The

people who come here are society enough not to care. My folks come here sometimes," Ricky said.

The inside of the hotel was very much as Sophie had pictured it: large, dark, gloomy rooms, glass enclosed porches with wicker furniture. The echo of hundreds of lazy summers spent within its aristocratic walls pervaded the atmosphere.

The few guests that they saw were families, tall, thin, tweedy families with well-behaved children and soft-spoken parents. Sophie's grandmother would call them a *goyish* group.

Ricky led her into the large dining room. Most of the tables were bare, and those few that were set for dining were against the windows facing the sea. The maître d'hôtel seated them at one. They ordered a tremendous sea-food dinner, which they enjoyed enormously.

"This has been a marvelous afternoon and evening," Sophie said, when they were having their coffee. It was dark out and the wind had become stronger; the sound of the sea and the wind outside lent an eerie quality to the large, almost empty dining room.

"It would be nice if we could stay here for the week-end," Ricky said.

Sophie laughed. "Yes, it would."

"Maybe someday we'll come back."

Sophie glanced up and met Ricky's eyes. "I doubt it," she said.

"Don't be so sure. Anything is possible. We might be married someday."

"I doubt it very much," Sophie said quietly.

Ricky didn't pursue the subject further, and the reminder of the problems between them cast a momentary gloom over Sophie's spirits. But she put those thoughts aside and started talking about something else quickly.

After dinner they explored the public rooms and porches on the main floor of the hotel, at last coming back to the desk to look at the movie notices. They were standing there when a young couple came in—a bright-looking boy and a pretty girl. The girl was wearing a corsage and the suitcase the boy was carrying was brand-new. Sophie nudged Ricky, and murmured, "Honeymooners."

Sophie watched the couple with frank curiosity. "They're adorable," she whispered to Ricky. "I want to wait until he registers. I bet he never signed Mr. and Mrs. before. The girl looks kind of scared, doesn't she?"

"Not at all," Ricky whispered back. "Just eager. Come on." He took her arm.

Sophie wanted to stay and watch them, but she could see that her curiosity was embarrassing Ricky. Slowly she followed him out. They were standing in front of the hotel taking a last look at the ocean, when to Sophie's surprise the young couple came out again, the boy still carrying the suitcase. They walked right toward them, and Sophie realized she was leaning against their car. The boy was clearly upset. "Those idiots," he said in an angry voice.

"We should have made a reservation," the girl's voice was low and gentle.

"Lot of good that would have done! No one needs a reservation this time of year. I know they have plenty of rooms!"

"But of course there's room. The place is almost empty." Sophie spoke up. She couldn't help herself.

"Not for people whose name is Levy," the boy said curtly, brushing past Sophie. "If you don't mind I'd like to get into my car."

Sophie was mortified. She stepped out of the way quickly. "I'm sorry. I'm terribly sorry."

The boy slammed the car door shut and started up his motor with a roar.

Sophie felt as if she wanted to fall through the ground. "Oh, Ricky." She turned a stricken face to him. "Isn't that awful?"

"It's terrible," Ricky agreed.

"Let's get out of here. I wish I hadn't eaten their dinner. It makes me sick."

"It's one of those things," Ricky said. "Just a dumb clerk who doesn't know any better."

Sophie's anger and disgust with the incident turned against Ricky in a sudden burst. "Don't you defend them. You never should have brought me here."

"How would I know?" Ricky was hurt. "It's not my fault."

"I suppose not. Come on. Let's go."

"Okay, okay." Ricky opened the car door for her and got in himself on the driver's side. "Don't take it out on me. I'm on your side."

Sophie didn't answer. She didn't want to get into a discussion with Ricky now. The incident had left her shaken and hurt, as if she had been physically bruised, inside and out. She felt apart from Ricky, apart from everyone. All she wanted was to be home, in her own room, in her own bed. She knew that Ricky felt indignant about what had happened too, yet she also felt sure that he wasn't affected as she was. Nothing had ever made her react this way before, and the strength of her emotions frightened her.

She kept thinking of the young couple all the way home. Where had they gone? What were they feeling? What were they saying to each other? What a way to start a marriage. . . .

She said good night to Ricky quickly and ran upstairs to

her room. Alone in her bed she cried, but she didn't know truly what she was crying about, whether it was for the indignity to the young honeymooners or for herself.

VII

Sophie hesitated in front of her grandfather's store before she walked in. She had avoided it, because she felt self-conscious there; the salesgirls made her uncomfortable with their smiles and fussing over "the boss's granddaughter." But she needed a few things for school, and her mother had said that going anywhere else was ridiculous, especially since the post-Thanksgiving sale was on.

Sophie had forced herself to stop thinking about the

incident at the hotel. She had not mentioned it to anyone, not even Patti, because she found it too painful and humiliating even to think about. To a degree she made herself accept Ricky's rationale that what had happened was merely the isolated ignorance of a dumb clerk.

"Sophie, come here." Her grandfather beckoned to her from the back of the store. She was surprised to find him chatting with Mr. Taylor. "You know my friend, Mr. Taylor?" Mr. Golden asked her.

Sophie nodded. "Yes, we've met."

"Indeed we have." Mr. Taylor's voice was quite genial. "I guess I'd better be going along. Step in any time you want to, Sam. The papers will be ready for you. Just sign your name, and you can have all the money you want."

"Thank you. Thank you very much." Mr. Golden's hand was outstretched, and the two men shook hands heartily.

After Mr. Taylor left, Sophie turned to her grandfather in amazement. "I didn't know you two were friends," she said.

Mr. Golden laughed. "Eric Taylor and I have been friends for years."

"But I thought he was supposed to be so anti-Semitic." Sophie was confused.

"We're friends in business. I borrow money from the

95

bank when I need to build up my inventory. My interest is as good as anyone's." He turned to Sophie. "I don't want to mix into your affairs. You're a young girl and you want to have a good time, but take some advice from an old man. I've lived in this town for many years, and I get along good with everyone because I know where I'm wanted and where I'm not. I don't push myself anywhere. I don't care that they don't want me to join the country club. Who needs it? Taylor and I understand each other, and we get along."

"I'm not trying to push myself into any group." Sophie spoke earnestly. She was shocked by her grandfather's calm acceptance of a situation that appalled her *if* it were true. She kept wondering, though, if the older people like her grandfather imagined the discrimination or if it really existed. Had that young couple really been turned away because their name was Levy . . . ?

Mr. Golden shrugged. "It's none of my business, but I hear you've got yourself a nice blond Aryan boyfriend. You're young and you should have a good time, but why did you pick him out?"

"Isn't he the son of a friend of yours, Mr. Taylor?" Sophie demanded.

Mr. Golden smiled and put his arm around Sophie. "You're a smart girl. But remember, there are all kinds of friends. I don't invite Mr. Taylor to my house, and he doesn't invite me to his. Our friendship is a different kind. And believe me, neither one of us forgets that."

"Maybe things are different now. Don't forget, Grandpa, my mother married a Gentile."

Mr. Golden smiled sadly. "Yes, I know. And your father's a fine man; I love him like I love my own sons. But your mother could have been happy with a Jewish husband too. What happened once doesn't have to happen again."

"Don't worry, I'm not marrying Ricky." Sophie laughed. "We're just going out together, Grandpa. That's all."

After Sophie bought what she wanted she left the store. The conversation with her grandfather was disturbing, but a more immediate problem was pressing on her mind. She would be talking to Ricky on the phone that night, and she knew that he would press her for an answer about joining the YF. The following Saturday they were all going to Boston, to a museum and a concert, and he wanted her to come too. She wanted to say yes, but she shrank from the storm her acceptance would raise at home. Fighting and more fighting . . . she was tired of the fights, but she was determined not to give up Ricky.

When Sophie arrived home she was surprised to find her mother baking a *challah,* the bread for the Sabbath.

"Aren't we going to Grandma's for dinner?" That was the usual Friday night custom.

"Yes, but I thought I'd bake a bread. I haven't done it for ages. Maybe you'd like to learn how one of these days." Mrs. Barnes's arms were immersed in flour as she kneaded the dough.

"No, thank you." Sophie examined her mother's noncommittal face. "You never used to bake. How come you're doing it now?"

"I just wanted to." She stopped what she was doing and looked up at her daughter. "I've been wrong, Sophie, in letting everything go, in not keeping up my own traditions and customs. It's too easy to forget who and what you are. I should have taught you more."

"If you're doing this for me, Mom, I'm not impressed. This whole business about being Jewish is silly. I'm an American, and that's enough for me."

"Who's an American? There are Italian-Americans, Irish-Americans, German-Americans. A Puerto Rican's an American too, but he's still called a Puerto Rican. And a Jew is a Jew. I don't use the labels; it's the people you call American who do. You're living in the world as it exists today, not in some Utopian society. And I don't care if I'm called a Jew; I'm not ashamed of it as you seem to be."

"Here we go again," Sophie murmured. "I'm tired of

98

being preached at. I am not you, and that's all there is to it. You may as well know right now that I'm thinking of joining the YF. I'm going to Boston with them on Saturday to a concert." Sophie looked at her mother defiantly. She had meant to bring up the subject at the right moment, and she was angry with herself for blurting it out now.

Her father had come into the kitchen, and she watched her mother turn to him with a helpless look on her face.

"Why the YF?" Mr. Barnes asked. "What made you pick that group?"

"Because my friends are in it." Sophie returned her father's look with steady eyes.

"You mean Ricky," her mother said. "You don't have any friends except Ricky and Patti, and I don't think Patti belongs. What's the matter with the Community Center?"

"I don't like it. That's what's the matter." Sophie stared at both her parents.

"You never gave it a chance," Mrs. Barnes said.

"I don't object to the YF." Mr. Barnes spoke deliberately. "But I'm very suspicious of your reason for wanting to join them. I'm afraid it's an anti-Semitic reason. If it were the only youth group around here, I'd feel different. But there happens to be a choice."

"And I choose the YF. What's so wrong with that?" Sophie demanded.

"The only thing wrong is your wanting to identify your-self with a church group in this community. Whether you like it or not, in this town you are a Jewish girl, and Jewish girls belong to the Community Center. You don't have to join anything, but to pick the YF is to push your-self in where you are not wanted. I don't like it." Mr. Barnes's face was troubled.

"I'm sorry if you don't like it, but that's what I'm going to do." Sophie picked up the packages she had put on the kitchen counter and stalked out of the room.

Upstairs she found herself shaking from the emotional tensions. They were not going to order her around. She was a person in her own right. She didn't have to accept their outmoded values and their imaginary fears.

Sophie sank down on her bed exhausted. The image of the young couple outside the hotel flashed across her mind, and she tried to shake it off. Her grandfather's words had stung her hard: "You've got yourself a nice blond Aryan boyfriend." She refused to believe that this background was Ricky's attraction for her, and yet she knew that when she was with him she was always a little conscious of what a handsome couple they made: the two tall, slim blond persons. With Ricky, no one would ever take her for a Jew. Sophie shivered, but her head felt hot and heavy.

Was it wrong to dislike being labeled? To refuse to accept the limitations of a kind of ghetto? America is a free country, Sophie told herself, and I'm going to make use of its freedom. When Ricky called, she said she would meet him on Saturday, although she did not commit herself to joining the group permanently.

That evening, at her grandmother's house, Sophie was very quiet. She paid careful attention to the ceremony of the Friday night Sabbath. She stood close to her grandmother when with a shawl covering her bowed head Mrs. Golden murmured her prayers over the lighted candles. At the dinner table Sophie listened attentively to her grandfather, with his hat on his head, saying the Hebrew prayer over the *challah* covered by a napkin. She knew in general what he was saying, because her grandfather had explained to her what the ritual meant. The ceremony was joyful, blessing the light that the candles made when sundown brought darkness, the bread and the wine that was drunk with it, and welcoming the Sabbath when no work was to be done. "It is not so different from what the Gentiles do when they say grace," her grandfather had once told her.

But why didn't she *feel* anything? If she was a Jew she wanted to *feel* being a Jew, and the prayers said in a hurried, singsong voice meant nothing to her. What did

101

being a Jew mean, if you didn't feel yourself one? Even her grandmother had said as much.

The dinner table was as gay as always. Her grandmother bounced up and down bringing in hot dishes, the uncles and aunts spoke with their usual exuberance, and, as it had of late, the talk inevitably turned to Uncle Harry's running for the school board. At this point everyone got excited, and the conversation took so many quick turns that Sophie hardly could follow it. No one was able to finish a sentence before he was interrupted. Her father was the only one who commanded silence and got it. Did they respect him more because he was the principal of the school or because he was a Gentile? Sophie suddenly wondered about her father's position in the family. He seemed very much at ease and at home, and yet he was a little different. He was more reserved and formal in his manner, his humor was not as warm or as ironic as the Goldens', he did not have their ability to mock both Mrs. Taylor and themselves. Were the differences there because he was Gentile and they were Jewish, or because he came from an Anglo-Saxon background and they from central Europe?

Sophie thought of all the blood mixed in her veins— English, Scottish, Russian, German, and maybe some Polish too—yet she only felt herself to be American and wanted to let her identification go at that.

"You're so quiet, Sophie," her grandmother said.

"She's thinking about her boyfriend," Aunt Sara remarked.

"That boy!" Her grandmother spoke with disgust and darted a look at Sophie's mother. Mrs. Barnes shook her head helplessly, her face crumpling under her mother's scornful expression.

Sophie flushed with embarrassment. "I wasn't thinking about anyone," she said. Suddenly she felt like crying. That she didn't *feel* Jewish, or that her mother had disappointed her grandmother, was not her fault. Her anger and frustration lay like an undigested lump of food in her stomach.

The next morning, when Sophie first woke up, she felt happy and excited. It was Saturday and she could see from her bed that the sun was shining. The day was going to be bright, cold, and crisp, and she was going to have all of it with Ricky. She started planning what she would wear: her plaid tweed suit, a turtleneck sweater, and her camel's hair coat. The outfit was British-looking, and she knew Ricky liked it. The YF girls weren't all that well dressed—some of them wore good clothes although they lacked style—but Sophie wanted to look particularly stunning today. Yes, she hoped to impress them. She was quite conscious of her motive—and so what? She wanted Ricky to be proud of her, which, she told herself, was a perfectly normal desire.

By the time she had taken her shower, however, a familiar hard knot was forming in her stomach. She still had to face her parents at breakfast before she took off. And the day had not begun auspiciously. First she had dropped a jar of cold cream on the bathroom floor—picking up all those tiny pieces was tiresome—and then she had torn a hole in her new textured stockings.

Before she went downstairs she tried to calm down. There is no point in being nervous she repeated to herself, concentrating on the thought while she was brushing her hair. Yet this step was a more drastic defiance of her parents. Going with Ricky had been one form of rebellion and independence, but going with him and to the YF was widening the gulf between them even more. She could imagine all the discussion and bemoaning that was going to go on among her mother and her grandmother and aunts.

Her parents were seated at the dining-room table when she came downstairs, and she could see by the expressions on their faces that they had been talking about her. "I see you're planning to go to Boston today," her mother said. "I wish we could persuade you to change your mind."

"You act as if I were doing something criminal. I'm only going to a museum and a concert. I should think you'd be glad I'm being so intellectual. And these kids are not a bunch of Hippies." Sophie giggled nervously. "They're a respectable church group."

"We are not objecting to the young people," Mr. Barnes said. "I'm sure they're perfectly nice. We simply don't trust your reason for picking them out. Heaven knows, I don't believe any group, Jews or anyone else, should stick together and not mix. But I can't help but be suspicious of your motives. If you didn't avoid the Jewish girls and boys so carefully, it would be different."

"I think you're making a big fuss over nothing. You're reading things into this that do not exist. Can't we talk about something else?" Sophie drank her orange juice and poured herself a cup of coffee.

"There are plenty of things to talk about," Mrs. Barnes said tartly, "but we cannot brush this situation aside."

"There is no situation," Sophie said angrily. "You're making one. The two of you are. It wasn't my idea to move to this town, and I think I'm making the best of a bad time. First you accused me of moping, and now that I'm trying to make some friends, you don't like them. You want everything your way. You want me to be happy here and to like the people that you like. Well I don't and that's that."

"On the surface what you say sounds very logical." Mr. Barnes's voice was calm. "But you refuse to look deeper and examine yourself and what you're doing. There happens to be a very bad state of affairs in this town, and you pretend it doesn't exist. Believe me, it's been an eye-opener to me. What are your values anyway? Just to have a good time for yourself. Don't you have any feeling of responsibility toward this community? How do you think it looks for a Jewish girl to be running around with the YF group and dating the son of the most anti-Semitic family in town?"

Sophie's face was pale, and her hand, holding her coffee cup, trembled. "Maybe I think I'm doing something constructive. You just said people should mix together instead of keeping apart. Why shouldn't I?"

Mr. Barnes smiled sadly. "You can't mix something that doesn't exist. You have to have an identity first. If you identified yourself clearly as a Jew, then you'd be free to go wherever you wanted, if you were welcome. That would be mixing. But you stand for nothing now, because you're ducking the issue; you're hoping these kids will accept you as a Barnes, not as a Golden. And we say that doesn't work. It never has and it never will."

"I'm sick of all this talk, and I've got to go." Sophie pushed her coffee cup away and got up from the table. "You can at least say you hope I'll have a good time," she said coldly.

"I hope you have a nice day," her mother said, but there were tears in her eyes.

Sophie took her coat and ran out of the house. She still had more than ten minutes to wait until Ricky picked her up, but she preferred being outside to sitting with her parents any longer. She felt that they were being wholly unfair and not giving her the benefit of the doubt.

"You look terrific," Ricky said, when he picked her up and drove to the church where the group was meeting. "I guess you've never been to a church before," Ricky said.

"Oh, but I have. I've gone with my grandparents, my father's parents. My grandfather was a minister before he retired."

That information seemed to make Ricky very happy. "No kidding, I never knew that. You could join this church, you know, if you wanted to."

Sophie felt herself grow tense. "I don't think I'd want to do that," she said. "I'm not very religious."

"Neither am I, but I go with my parents sometimes anyway." He was silent for a few minutes. "I just thought it might be a good idea."

They had reached the church now, but neither of them got out of the car. Some of the group were standing on the sidewalk, but not everyone was there so they weren't ready to leave yet. Sophie glanced at Ricky swiftly, and then looked away. "You mean your parents would forget that I'm part Jewish?" Sophie asked the question more as if she were stating a fact.

Ricky turned to her eagerly. "Look, you know that I don't give a hang what you are. I'm not with my parents on this stuff. But they've been giving me a hard time, and if you did join the church that would make you the same as everyone else. And with your grandfather having been a minister, it would seem perfectly natural. I mean, you don't seem any more of a Jew than I am."

Sophie was silent. Then she spoke slowly. "I could make myself like the people who belong to your church, but they're not the whole world, Ricky." Then she added in a gentler tone, "My parents have been giving me a hard time too. But we're not going to solve the problem now. Let's have a good time and forget it today."

"Sure thing." Ricky agreed, but she felt that he was disappointed in her reaction to his suggestion.

The day started out very well. The group was not a large one; five boys and seven girls piled into the minister's large station wagon. Sophie knew them all by sight from school, and while she felt an outsider that reaction seemed perfectly natural, since she had no more than a nodding acquaintance with any of them. At luncheon, however, Mr. Ives, the minister, began a discussion on a sermon he had given, and Sophie became aware of a religious overtone to the outing that left her uncomfortable. The conversation made her wince, and Ricky's sympathetic glances in her direction were no help. The end of lunch came as a relief, and they went on to the concert.

After the concert they walked around the Boston Common to a museum, and the girls stopped to look at the shop windows, already aglow with Christmas decorations and gifts. The talk naturally turned to Christmas. Sophie was walking with Ricky and a small, thin-faced girl named Elaine Whitney.

"It must be awful not to celebrate Christmas," Elaine said, turning to Sophie.

Sophie looked at her in surprise. "But we have Christmas. I've had a Christmas tree and presents ever since I can remember. What makes you think I don't?"

Elaine was embarrassed. "I didn't think Jews celebrated Christmas. Don't you have a holiday of your own?" There was a possessive, patronizing note in her voice, as if Sophie had no right to share in her Christmas.

"I suppose some Jewish people celebrate Chanukah, but my father isn't Jewish so we've always had Christmas," Sophie said quietly.

"It must be awful being half and half," Elaine said with a little laugh. "I'd hate that."

"It's not important," Sophie said curtly. They walked about a block before the idea hit Sophie that she wished she hadn't mentioned that her father wasn't Jewish. Her reply sounded as if she were apologizing for herself or bragging about him. She wanted to kick herself—and then she was so surprised at her own reaction that she dismissed the whole question. Why shouldn't she say that her father wasn't Jewish?

When they left the group at the church and she got into the car with Ricky, Sophie felt very tired. "Did you have a good time?" he asked. "You were awfully quiet on the way back."

"I enjoyed it. It was a nice day."

"You don't sound very enthusiastic. What's the matter? Don't you like the kids?"

"They're all right." Sophie felt Ricky's eyes on her, but she didn't turn around to face him.

"What's the matter? Out with it. You can't be angry at

110

Elaine's stupid remark. But you shut up after it." Ricky tried to turn her face around toward him.

Sophie finally looked up at him, but averted her face before she started to speak. "I guess I was bothered by the talk about Christmas and Jesus Christ. It went on all through lunch and all the way home. I suppose I thought they were deliberately excluding me. Christmas has never been a religious holiday for me. We just had Christmas because everyone else did. But of course we never went to church. My mother wouldn't dream of that. Sometimes I do wish I were one thing or the other!"

"You can be if you want," Ricky said gently. "You can choose what you want to be. You can join our church."

"Yes, I know," Sophie said morosely. "But I don't know if that's what I want."

Ricky started the car, and they drove to Sophie's house. "I don't suppose you want to go to a movie tonight?" Ricky sounded as if he knew the answer.

"No, I don't. Thanks, anyway. I'm tired. I think I'll go to bed early."

Sophie was tired, both from the excursion and from the emotional strain of the day. The occasion hardly had been worth fighting about with her parents, and yet if she hadn't gone, she would have been sorry. Sophie did go to bed early, but falling asleep took a long time. Her mind kept moving from one thing to another as she tossed and turned. Finally she took some headache pills and lulled herself to rest.

VIII

"Tell me about yesterday," Patti said to Sophie on Sunday afternoon.

"There's nothing much to tell. It was all right." Sophie didn't feel like talking about it. The day had been peculiar, but she couldn't put her finger on the reason. She had not had a bad time, but she had felt a stranger.

"You don't sound very enthusiastic," Patti commented. "All those Wasps too much for you?" she asked shrewdly.

"No, of course not. I'm used to that. Of course, everyone knew each other, and I didn't—but it was okay."

"There's a big dance at the Country Club next Saturday night. Has Ricky asked you to it?" Patti said.

"No, not yet," Sophie admitted.

When Sophie came home, however, there was a message that Ricky had called and she was to call him back.

When Sophie hung up the receiver, her mother asked what had happened because she looked upset.

"I'm not really upset," Sophie protested. Then, facing both her parents, she said, "I suppose I may as well tell you now as any time. Ricky invited me to a dance at the Country Club next Saturday night, and I'm going."

Her parents exchanged shocked glances. Mrs. Barnes threw up her hands in distress. "You talk to her, Peter. I give up."

"Let's keep calm," Mr. Barnes said to his wife soothingly. "If none of us gets excited, we can at least hear what each other is saying. Come on, Sophie. Let's sit down." He led his family into the living room and sat down in a large easy chair. Sophie and Mrs. Barnes sat at either end of the sofa.

"I want to ask you a question," Mr. Barnes said, addressing Sophie. "Why do you want to go to a dance at a place that even I wouldn't go to? You don't have to be a Jew not to condone anti-Semitism. Good Christians resign from clubs that bar anyone for racial reasons. No Jews are allowed to join the club. You know that?"

"I've heard it," Sophie said. "I have no way of knowing whether it's true or not."

"You'll have to take our word for that," Mr. Barnes said briskly.

"We all know it's true," Mrs. Barnes said. "I lived in this town until I got married. Your grandparents and aunts and uncles live here. We know it's true."

"I thought we were going to keep calm," Sophie said. "You're screaming at me already. Even if it is true, I don't know what that has to do with my going there for a dance one evening. If they hate Jews so much, why did Ricky's parents let him invite me? He told me on the phone that it was all right with them."

Mr. Barnes frowned. "I think I know why." His voice was calmer. "I have no way of proving this, Sophie, but I think Mrs. Taylor is using you. She is accused of being anti-Semitic, and your presence would help her say she is not. Her son took Sophie Barnes to a dance with them at the club; she thinks this will whitewash her."

Sophie was indignant. "You have a devious mind, and

you have no right to say such a thing. I think your whole assumption is ridiculous. I don't believe you, and it's not going to change my mind. I am going to the dance."

Mrs. Barnes was tense. "I am not going to sit here calmly and let you talk that way." She turned to Sophie. "We'll just have to forbid you to go to that dance, that's all. I don't care if you see the reasons or not, or agree or not. You can't go. That's the end of it."

"How are you going to stop me?" Sophie asked defiantly.

"Let's not get excited," Mr. Barnes repeated. "Your mother is emotional about this subject, and I can't blame her. Can't you see how terrible it would look for Uncle Harry, for everyone in this family, and for every Jew in Woodview if you went to a dance at that restricted club? The people at the club won't even respect you; you won't respect yourself, Sophie."

The strain was bringing Sophie to tears. "I can't stand this anymore. Can't any of you forget for one minute that you're Jews! You're *not* one," she said to her father accusingly.

"No, but I'm married to one, and my daughter is Jewish. Your grandmother told you that the line goes through the mother. If your mother is Jewish, you're a Jew, so forget this half business. I've learned in Woodview that there is no such a thing. Maybe someday, in some Utopia it will make no difference, but we're surely not there yet. In the meantime, people have to live together, but not at the expense of betraying their own kind, giving up their own customs and traditions in exchange for others. No, your grandmother is right. No one can forget that he is a Jew. I'm not Jewish, but I can see that."

"Thank heavens, you're the one saying these things," Mrs. Barnes said. "I *am* emotional about this, and I'm not ashamed to say so. I'd hate myself if I weren't!"

"You haven't any right to forbid me to go to a dance. You'll be sorry." Sophie glowered darkly. She stalked out of the room, trembling.

All kinds of wild thoughts raced through her mind. She was tempted to join the YF, to run away from home. . . . She wanted to do something desperate and dramatic to escape from the pressures. But she knew she wouldn't do any of them. She despised the situation, but she loved her parents, and actually she felt tragically helpless in the bind in which she was caught. There seemed to be no way to solve her dilemma.

Nothing was resolved. There was a block between Sophie and her parents that kept the tensions and strain alive between them. Sophie discussed her problem with Patti and then with Ricky. Patti was sympathetic, but she did say that she thought she could understand Sophie's mother's point of view. "My mother would have a fit if I didn't go to mass," Patti said. "But then," she added, "I was brought up that way from the beginning. My parents used to get awful mad when Kennedy was president and people said they didn't like a Catholic running the country. You do have to stick by your own people."

Sophie became more confused than ever. And when she spoke to Ricky, his argument was different. "Why not come to the dance?" he asked. "If your folks want to break down restrictions, maybe this is a way to start."

"My father says that restrictions would have to be lifted first. That to come this way would be sliding in the back door." She didn't want to tell him what her parents had said about Mrs. Taylor using her as a screen.

They discussed it back and forth until Ricky put his arms around her. "Don't I mean anything to you?" he asked her. "If I want you to come to the dance, because I like you so much and I don't care what you are, isn't that what counts? I mean, isn't it something just between you and me? We don't have to care what everyone else thinks."

Sophie rested her head against his shoulder. "Wouldn't that be wonderful? To forget the rest of the world and go off someplace by ourselves."

"Maybe we will," Ricky said, taking her in his arms. "Forget all about the turmoil going on in the world, everyone fighting with everyone else. You're not the only one who's in a mess. The whole world's a mess. We should start all over again from the beginning."

"But then we'd have to have everyone looking alike, thinking alike, dressing alike, or we'd be right back where we are now. That seems to be the choice—a world of robots or people who are different fighting with each other. There should be a better way."

"Well, one way," Ricky said, trying to cheer her up, "is for you and me to go to the dance on Saturday night. Let's show them all that we don't care."

"I'll have to think about it," Sophie said. Ricky's enthusiasm scared her off. Why did he care so much if she came to the club? When she thought about the question, she began to resent his invitation. In a way he was the one who had put her in this position, and although she would never in a million years say so to her parents, she suddenly became annoyed with him for having asked her to a place that did not welcome Jews. Why had he done such a stupid thing?

On Thursday Sophie made up her mind. She was not going to the dance, but she also was not going to give in to her parents and say they were right. The easiest thing, she decided, was to go away for the weekend. She hadn't been to New York since they had moved to Woodview, and now seemed an excellent time to go. A telephone call to her old friend Abbie settled the matter. Abbie was enthusiastic; she said that she was going to a big dance on Saturday night and that she'd get a date for Sophie.

Mr. and Mrs. Barnes were surprised when Sophie announced her plans, but they too welcomed her solution of the problem. The only one who didn't think it was a good idea was Ricky. He tried his best to talk Sophie out of going, but once she had arrived at a decision she stuck to it. She even went so far as to tell Ricky to take someone else to the dance, which suggestion made him all the angrier. He told Sophie that persuading his mother to agree to ask her had taken a long time, and that suddenly one day, much to his surprise, his mother had said yes. "I think I know why she did," Sophie told him, but she wouldn't give him her reason.

They patched up their disagreement, but Sophie felt that neither one of them would completely forget it.

When she got on the train Saturday, Sophie felt as if she had left all her cares behind her. It was a gray December morning, but she didn't care whether the sun was shining or not; she was going to her beloved New York. By the time Sophie emerged from Grand Central Station, the sun had come out, and as she walked over to Madison Avenue for the uptown bus to Abbie's house she felt as if she had completely shed herself of Woodview.

The city was ready for Christmas, the stores bright and gay with decorations, the Salvation Army ladies singing their doleful hymns on street corners, and the crowds smiling and laden with bundles. Sophie wanted to take the people in her arms and hug them. How marvelous to see chic girls and dark-skinned people on the streets and to listen to the language of the city. Woodview might as well be on another planet.

Sophie felt as if she were coming home when she stepped into the somber but elegant lobby of Abbie's Fifth Avenue apartment. Abbie welcomed her with open arms.

"I'm dying to hear all about you," she said, and without waiting for an answer went headlong into a tale about her new boyfriend, Tommy De Vries, all the parties she'd been going to, and her big debutante ball that was going to take place in the spring. "You'll have to come to it. It'll be terrific. Now tell me about you."

"There's not much to tell," Sophie said. She described Ricky to Abbie, pretty much repeating what she had written to her, but when she had finished there wasn't much more to say. Sophie did not want to go into the problems of Woodview or into her own troubles with her family and the whole Jewish conflict. In fact, Abbie probably didn't even know that she *was* Jewish. This realization gave Sophie an odd feeling, as if she were playing a role on the stage or leading a double life. She thought of her grandmother, of the Friday night candles, the matzoh-ball soup and the *gefilte* fish, and she wondered what Abbie would think of the household. "Oh, yes . . . what did you say?" Sophie had hardly been listening to Abbie's chatter.

"I was telling you about your date for tonight. He's not terribly good-looking, but he's really sweet. His name is Johnny Rittenhouse. He comes from an awfully good family." Abbie was concentrating on trimming a pair of false eyelashes.

"All your friends come from 'awfully good families,' " Sophie commented.

Abbie looked at her curiously. "That's a queer thing to say. What do you mean?"

Sophie shrugged. "Nothing. It's true, isn't it?"

Abbie made a sound that wasn't quite a laugh. "But of course. Don't yours?"

"I suppose." Sophie looked out the window with an absent-minded expression on her face. Then she pulled herself together with an effort. She was here to have a good time and to get away from her problems, so there was no sense in mooning about them.

Johnny Rittenhouse turned out to be a pale-faced boy with glasses; he had a warm smile and a dry sense of humor. "This dance is going to be a terrible drag," he announced to Sophie in the taxi going over. "The girls are going to dance with their fathers and the boys with their mothers. Thank goodness, my mother is in Europe and I never see my father. I suggest we give it one hour, sixty minutes, and then bomb out to a discotheque."

Abbie and Sophie giggled. "Good idea," Abbie's date agreed. He was a tall, good-looking boy, who spoke in a soft voice and had beautiful manners.

Johnny's prediction about the dance, although exaggerated, wasn't far from wrong. There were too many chaperones, and it was dull. Sophie thought that watching the girls, all dressed up in their long dresses, and the boys, in dark suits or tuxedos, having such a dreary time was sad. If this affair was typical of a society dance, it wasn't for her.

Exactly an hour after they arrived, Johnny herded the four of them plus another couple off to a discotheque nearby. They went into a small room crowded with young people dancing. The music was loud and wild, and the couples were packed so close together everyone had to stay in his own little spot on the dance floor. It was so totally different from the place they had left that the six of them felt exhilarated.

"No inhibitions here," Johnny commented.

"It's marvelous." Sophie loved the noise of the conversation, the sound of the throbbing music, the informal, free atmosphere. They were the only group in evening clothes, but no one paid any attention, every one was too busy having a good time. This was New York, this was the kind of excitement Sophie had been missing. She faced Johnny on the dance floor, and the two of them fell into the rhythm of the music.

When finally there was a break, the three couples sat at a small table. The room was so noisy they could barely hear each other speak.

"This is a marvelous place. I love it," Sophie said enthusiastically. She hadn't felt this relaxed in months. Woodview was for the moment forgotten.

"It used to be better," Abbie's friend Dina said. "Before the Jews took over."

Sophie's heart stood still. She turned cold and then felt burning hot. "What's the matter with the Jews?" she heard her own voice asking. She sounded like a stranger, the words were spoken automatically as if someone else were controlling her vocal cords.

Dina turned to her with surprise. "I don't like them in hordes, that's all. Hope I haven't stepped on anybody's toes," she added lightly.

Abbie laughed. "No one here is Jewish."

"It so happens that my mother is Jewish," Sophie said flatly. There was a dead silence at the table.

"Oh, well, that's different," Dina said cooly.

"My mother's Irish, and I guess that's just as bad," Johnny said with a good-natured laugh. "Come on, Sophie, let's dance," he said, as the music started up.

Sophie turned to him gratefully, but she caught a glimpse of Abbie's closed-up, remote face as she left.

"I should have kept my mouth shut," Sophie said to Johnny on the dance floor.

"Forget it. Dina's a big snob. And she's stupid besides."

"I don't care about Dina. I was thinking of Abbie. She never knew that I was half-Jewish."

"It's not going to hurt her," Johnny said. "It's good for her to know someone out of that little closed circle of hers. Just forget it."

Sophie wished that she could forget the scene, but she couldn't. Abbie kept her eyes averted from her for the rest of the evening, and Sophie dreaded the balance of her visit.

When the two girls were alone in Abbie's bedroom later that night, Sophie felt the strain between them. "I'm sorry if what I said upset you." Sophie said. "I suppose I shouldn't have spoken so directly, but I couldn't help it."

Abbie's face was still remote. "I think it's very funny that you never mentioned it before."

"I know," Sophie said. "It never came up, that's all. I'm sorry if it troubles you," she added in a cold voice.

Abbie swung around, her face distorted with fury. "Don't you start pinning labels on me. You were the one who was apparently ashamed of being Jewish, not me. I couldn't care less what you are," she added haughtily.

Sophie lay in bed awake for a long time. She was experiencing a curious kind of elation from the events of the evening, but also a great deal of uncertainty. Tonight was the first time in her life that she had ever taken a stand about being a Jew, and she wasn't sure whether she felt proud or silly. Some part of her thought that she had acted with honesty and dignity, and yet she also wondered whether she should have kept her mouth shut. Certainly she had alienated Abbie, and yet, she argued with herself, if Abbie felt the way she did, what value was her friendship? Was this the beginning of a whole new phase of her life? The idea frightened Sophie. She was not prepared to start battling about being a Jew, and yet she did draw satisfaction and relief from having taken a position. She was reacting as though she had got rid of a headache or some vague unpleasantness that had hovered over her.

The next day neither one of the girls mentioned their words or the events of the evening before. However, when Sophie suggested that she take an early train home, Abbie did not coax her to stay. And on her return, Sophie could not help but smile to herself when she remembered that not another word had been mentioned about the invitation to Abbie's coming-out party.

IX

On the following Wednesday, Sophie came to her father's office at the elementary school to meet him for a ride home. She was shocked to find him slumped at his desk with his head in his hands. "What's the matter?" she asked. When he raised his head, she saw how haggard his face had become and she noticed little wrinkles around his eyes and mouth that she was sure were new.

"Look at this." He handed her a crudely mimeographed

letter. It was addressed "Dear Voter," and it was a scurrilous attack on both her Uncle Harry and her father. It accused her Uncle Harry of having brought in his "atheist" brother-in-law as principal in order to undermine the Christian beliefs of the schoolchildren and spoke of a "clique of Jews and atheists, who are working together to control the school and subvert the children." It was signed anonymously "A Group of Concerned Christian-American Parents."

"That's hideous. What brought this on?" Sophie asked. She dropped the sheet hastily.

"At the school-board meeting Monday night I said I didn't think we should have a religious Christmas play. I said I thought that belonged in a church and not in a public school. I think that precipitated this letter. They sure didn't waste any time." Mr. Barnes picked up the paper and stared at it. "It's filthy, isn't it? It also scares me." He looked up at Sophie. "This country is full of violence. The racial conflict in town has brought out the best and the worst in people, and the worst, as usual, is becoming more anti-Semitic."

"What are you going to do?"

"What can we do? Hope that the town's good sense will not accept this kind of smear. Work like the devil to get Harry elected, although I'm not very optimistic."

"I think this letter is ghastly, but what's wrong with a religious play for Christmas? We always had one at school." Sophie was shocked by the letter, but she didn't understand her father's position.

"I don't think it's right. There are Jewish kids in school, and maybe some parents don't have a religion. I don't believe a religious play belongs in a public school, and I said so." Mr. Barnes's face was grim. "Your boyfriend's mother hit the ceiling; she got very nasty. The board voted me down, but that doesn't make them right."

"Then there will be a Christmas play?"

Mr. Barnes nodded. "Yes."

Sophie was very quiet on the ride home. She was badly frightened and wondered if there would ever be an end to the hideous strife in which she was trapped. Her life had seemed so simple and easy before they moved to Woodview, and she longed for the good old carefree days. She had not mentioned the incident at the discotheque to anyone, but she was aware that every time she thought of it a warm feeling welled up in her because she had spoken up. It almost blocked out the memory of the unpleasantness.

It was two weeks before Christmas, and Sophie realized that there were no signs of Christmas in her own house.

Usually by this time a lot of sparkling Christmas paper and ribbons were piled up in a corner of the living room, mysterious packages were hidden behind coats in the closet, and various decorative objects that were saved from year to year appeared out of tissue paper and boxes.

Sophie mentioned the lack of Christmas preparations at the dinner table that night and immediately caught the exchange of glances between her parents. Her heart sank with a terrible suspicion.

"Your father and I have been talking about it," Mrs. Barnes said uneasily. "It so happens that this year Chanukah comes at around the same time as Christmas. As a matter of fact, it starts two days before, on the twenty-third, and we thought we should celebrate it with the rest of the family."

Sophie was dumfounded. "No Christmas!" She couldn't believe her ears. "But we've always had Christmas."

"Christmas is for children. You're a big girl now." Her father tried to force a smile.

"But why? Why? I love Christmas. It's . . . it's a national holiday. Everyone celebrates Christmas. Why suddenly no Christmas?" Sophie could not comprehend that they were serious.

"Not everyone does celebrate Christmas," Mrs. Barnes said gently. "I'm afraid I'm the one responsible for this. I can understand how you feel, Sophie, but it's mainly my mother and father that I'm thinking of. They'd be very upset if they saw a Christmas tree here. . . ."

"No Christmas tree!" Sophie was shocked.

"It was different when we lived in New York. What they didn't know, or see, didn't hurt them. But now—especially with all the struggle that's going on in this town—well, they'd think we were traitors if we celebrated Christmas." Mrs. Barnes looked at Sophie beseechingly. "I know this is a terrible blow for you. But Chanukah is fun, and you get presents, lots of presents. Every day for eight days you'll have a present."

"I don't care about Chanukah." Sophie pushed her plate away. "Maybe I sound like a baby, but I don't care. I'm going to get my own Christmas tree and put it up in my room. I don't want any Chanukah presents. Christmas is not a religious holiday to me; it's something we've always done together, the three of us. I think you two are mean to give it up." She looked at her mother with blazing eyes. "You're not living with your mother and father. You're living here, in this house with Daddy and me. And if we want Christmas I think we should have it."

Mrs. Barnes's face was pale and tears were wetting her cheeks. "I didn't think you'd take it so hard. I wish I knew what was right and what was wrong."

"I don't think the issue here is whether Christmas is a religious holiday for us or not," Mr. Barnes said soberly. "The point is we have had a Christmas every year. Can we make a sacrifice this year so as not to offend your grandparents, who are not so young anymore?" He was looking at Sophie thoughtfully. "The second thing we have to decide is where we stand in this community. There is obviously an anti-Semitic drive on. It is pointed against us, and especially against Esther's family, as well as the rest of the Jews. Wouldn't we be wiser and stronger to stand by the Jewish tradition of Chanukah and just skip Christmas?"

Sophie ran her hand through her blond hair nervously. "You make it sound so logical. But Christmas isn't something logical; it's something you *feel*," she wailed. "I'll never *feel* Chanukah!"

"Maybe sometime you will," her mother said. "If you give it a chance, and if you ever start *feeling* like a Jew."

As usual after one of their discussions, Sophie could see that nothing was resolved, nothing solved. She continued to act as before, and they went on talking as before. She was in absolute despair. The thought also occurred to her that she hadn't heard from Ricky for the past two days. He usually made a point of getting together with her in school or of phoning her in the evening. She was feeling blue enough to decide to call him.

His voice sounded odd to her on the phone, but he insisted she was imagining things, and he agreed to meet her in half an hour. Sophie had a great sense of foreboding as she washed her face and brushed her hair, but she put it down to her general gloom.

In a little while she heard his horn outside.

"Come on in. Let's go for a ride." Ricky leaned over and opened the door for her. "What's the matter?" he asked.

"Why? Do I look awful?" Sophie pulled down the mirror in his car to examine her face. "Yes, I do."

"I've seen you look better. You look upset."

"Upset! I'm in a state," Sophie said. She told him about the fight she'd had with her parents over Christmas. "It's so ridiculous," she ended up. "They're trying to turn me into something that I'm not."

Ricky looked at her sympathetically. "I think it's time you were what you wanted to be. I was going to lead up to this gracefully, but I'm not the type. I've been thinking about you, and I think it's time you chucked all this in-between stuff, took my advice, and joined my church."

Sophie was jolted. This response was not what she had expected. She shook her head negatively. "Oh, I couldn't do that. What good would that do anyway?"

Ricky was embarrassed. "It would be easier, that's why."

There was something in Ricky's voice and manner that renewed Sophie's premonition of an unpleasant experience.

"Easier for whom? Ricky, tell me what's up. I have a feeling that something's going on that I won't like." Sophie looked out of the car at the cold, winter scene. The houses they passed appeared warm and snug with their Christmas decorations and lights. Some of them had an elaborate Santa Claus on the chimney or Nativity scenes on the lawn, and a few had outdoor decorated Christmas trees. Sophie experienced a pang of jealousy for the security behind these displays. The people in those houses had no uncertainty about where they belonged or who they were, and they were not shy about letting the world know what their faith was.

"Apparently something happened at the school board meeting Monday night that set my mother off. She doesn't want me to see you anymore." Ricky was looking straight ahead at the road while he spoke. When he finished he gave her a sidelong glance.

"I know what happened at the school board." She was not completely surprised by what Ricky had to say, yet the words lay like a dull lump between them. For a while they drove in silence, and then Ricky took hold of her hand and tried to pull her closer to him. But Sophie pulled away and stayed on her side of the seat.

"Don't pull away from me," Ricky said sharply. "My mother can't stop me from seeing you. Don't be ridiculous."

"I've got to think about it," Sophie said. "I'm trying to figure out the connection between your mother and your wanting me to join the church."

Ricky shrugged. "I thought it would make everything easier."

"But I'd still be what I am. If your mother hates me because I'm half a Jew, my joining the church wouldn't change that, would it?"

"Of course, it would. You'd be making your choice and not be Jewish," Ricky said.

Sophie bristled. "But that's stupid! I'm Jewish because my mother is, and nothing can change that. You can't undo how you were born. Ricky, you don't like me being Jewish either, do you?" She put the question to him softly.

Ricky pulled the car to a stop. They were on a hill overlooking the town. "It makes for complications," he said gruffly. Then he pulled Sophie to him and kissed her hard on the mouth. "I'm crazy about you," he said, "and I don't give a hang what you are. But I also have to live with my family."

Sophie clung to him for a few minutes. She liked the clean smell of him and the soft wool of his sweater against her cheek. She could not give him up. At that moment she loved him more than anyone in the world. He was also her only connection with a life that she knew and wanted to be part of. To leave him would be cutting herself off from a whole free and open world, and at the same time she would be making a commitment to a world that frightened her: a dark world in which she would be someone apart, someone different, a world inhabited by people with strange ways and customs, people with a long anguished history of being unwanted and homeless, of being tormented and molested, put to death in pogroms and gas chambers. Sophie shivered in Ricky's arms.

"I can't do it," she sobbed. "I can't join a church. I would never feel right, and it would kill my mother."

Ricky held her close to him. "Forget it. I guess the

suggestion was stupid at that. Don't cry, baby. I'll figure something out."

Sophie pulled herself away from him. There was a look of amazement on her face. "How can we not see each other?" she asked. "We'll see each other in school every day. We're bound to meet all the time."

"Of course. I know." Ricky nodded. "My mother meant dating, but don't worry," he added hastily. "We'll work something out."

When Sophie came back to her house that night she was desolate. All of Ricky's reassuring words were lost in the fog of gloom that enveloped her. This evening was the beginning of the end as far as she and Ricky were concerned; she was sure of that. She couldn't bear the thought of living in Woodview all the months until the end of the school year, all during the summer, until she went to college in the fall, without him. The town would be worse than a jail. They would see each other constantly and yet not see each other at all.

The four walls of her room seemed to be closing in on her. No exit. She was trapped and without a friend in the world. Abbie was out, Ricky was on his way, and there were some things she could not talk to Patti about. The main thing was this awful fear that hung over her. Her very awareness of it frightened her, the fear of what Ricky stood for and why she wanted it so much. Was she afraid of being a Jew? The idea nauseated her, filled her with a feeling of self-disgust.

Sophie got undressed and crawled into bed, burying her head deep under the covers. To sleep and sleep, forget all her problems, wake up with them gone . . . and finally she did fall into a heavy, deep sleep.

X

Each day as Christmas drew closer, and the gaiety and excitement of the Christmas season mounted, Sophie's torment became worse. Everything that she would have loved, the lights on Main Street, the big silver Christmas tree on the square, the smell of snow in the air and wood-fires burning, the smiles on people's faces, every shop-keeper saying "Merry Christmas," all added to her un-happiness. She felt as if she had dropped from another planet into a world that was intent on excluding her from its affairs.

One afternoon she bought a tiny, artificial Christmas tree and set it up in her room. But it looked so forlorn and lonely that it made her even sadder. She knew that her parents were buying her presents, Chanukah presents, but the thought was more irritating than cheering.

Four days before Christmas Sophie made up her mind what she wanted to do. Without discussing the matter with her parents, she called up her Grandmother Barnes in Brooklyn and asked if she could come to spend Christmas with them. They were overjoyed by the idea, and as soon as she hung up the phone Sophie's spirits rose. That evening at dinner she told her mother and father that she was going down to her grandparents the next day.

Mrs. Barnes was troubled, but Sophie's father was amused by the way she had solved her problem about Christmas.

"You'll have to wait another day, for the first night of Chanukah," Mrs. Barnes said. "Your grandparents here will be very disappointed if you're not with them. That way you'll have both Chanukah and Christmas," Mrs. Barnes said brightly.

"Do I have to?" Sophie looked to her father.

"Yes, I think that's a good idea," he said.

141

The snow came during the first afternoon of the Chanukah celebration. Sophie watched it from her window as she was getting ready for the evening. Ever since she had decided to go to Brooklyn for Christmas she had been feeling considerably better, and the sight of the large, white snowflakes falling on the frozen ground put her in a holiday mood. Her mother had told her to look pretty, so she dressed in a short, black velvet skirt and a flattering white, frilly blouse. She brushed her blond hair until it shone and clipped on her best, old garnet earrings.

"You look lovely," her mother said, when she came downstairs. Sophie returned the compliment to Mrs. Barnes, who wore a becoming red wool dress. For the first time in months Sophie and her parents were amiable and in tune with each other. I guess it's the holiday spirit, Sophie thought to herself, and wondered whether she was looking forward to Christmas or tonight's Chanukah.

The Goldens' house was ablaze with lights when the Barnes arrived. Grandma Golden was shining, her hair was perfectly waved, and she was wearing a black dress adorned by a single, stunning brooch set with what Sophie immediately assumed were diamonds. Mrs. Golden laughed. "They're paste, darling, paste." She hugged Sophie hard. "When my mother came to this

142

country she kept her diamonds in a vault. Every time she went to the opera she had to nag my father to get her lavalier—that's what it was called in those days—from the vault. Such commotion. Not for me. If I had diamonds I'd wear them, but who needs it? I'd worry myself sick."

All the family were already there. The aunts and uncles, Rachel and Dickie, and even Uncle Joe. "Come, have a little schnapps," Grandpa Golden said. He poured some whiskey into small glasses and handed them around. "It's a holiday. Happy Chanukah everyone. Let's drink to Harry, the first Jew who will be elected to the school board in Woodview."

Harry laughed. "Not so fast, Dad. I'm not elected yet."

His father slapped him on the back affectionately. "You have to have confidence. We have to drink to Dickie too. He'll have his *bar mitzvah* soon." He kissed his grandson's happy face lovingly.

The whiskey felt good to Sophie, coming in from the cold, and her tensions relaxed in the warmth of the room and the good-natured banter of her relatives. Only Uncle Joe remained in his own silence, and Sophie seated herself at the end of the room near him. She was still a little afraid of his austerity, but he fascinated her and she wished she could get to know him better.

"It's wonderful to have the whole family together. The

first Chanukah in so many years," Grandma Golden said, sighing with content. A soft look was exchanged between Mrs. Barnes and her mother that did not escape Sophie's eye. She realized how meaningful each family celebration and reunion was to her mother and her grandmother. Although the shadow of the earlier family rift that always brought a fleeting depression was still present, today it quickly was dispersed in the jovial holiday atmosphere.

"Come on, boys. Put on your hats. Dora's going to bring in the menorah." Only Uncle Joe wore the traditional little round, black skullcap. The other men put on their ordinary felt hats, and Dickie placed a beanie over his long haircut. Grandma Dora brought in the beautiful old silver menorah, the candle holder for the eight candles of Chanukah.

Sophie knew the story of Chanukah, because her mother had told her about it. She knew that long, long ago in the city of Modin, in Palestine, Judas Maccabaeus and his brothers fought a war against Antiochus and his armies. After Antiochus was defeated, Judas and his brothers were busy cleaning out the temple, which Antiochus had defiled, when the eternal light flickered and was about to go out. To Judas's horror, he saw that there was no oil left, and the eternal light must never go out. So Judas sent two of his brothers, the Maccabees "to beat the oil out of the olive trees" while Judas watched the one little lamp to keep it burning. He kept praying it would last until the oil came. The mission took eight days, and miraculously the light lasted until the Maccabees came back with the fresh oil. That is why Chanukah is called the Feast of the Lights.

Ceremoniously, Grandpa Golden lighted the first candle in the menorah. Then everyone kissed each other, and said, "Happy Chanukah." Both Sophie's mother and her grandmother seemed to be telling her how happy they were that she was there by their especially hard hugs. She was glad that she was there too.

There were small presents for Dickie, Rachel, and Sophie. The girls each received a scarf and blouse, a pair of earrings, and gay stockings. "Sometimes children get a small present each day," Grandma Golden explained to Sophie, "but you two are big girls so you don't need that."

"Mother said she had a present for me each day. I guess she wants to make up for not having Christmas," Sophie said.

"But I hear you won't be here the rest of the week. I guess you don't like Woodview very much." Mrs. Golden's eyes showed disappointment.

"I'm not crazy about Woodview," Sophie said frankly,

145

"but it's not that. I'd like to see my other grandparents too."

"Yes, of course," Mrs. Golden said, but the expression on her face belied her words. Suddenly the thought occurred to Sophie that Grandma Golden was very jealous of Sophie's other grandparents.

"Come with me," Mrs. Golden said to her. "I have a little something I want to give you." She took Sophie into her bedroom. One wall was covered with baby pictures of everyone in the family, and Sophie was surprised to see a familiar baby picture of herself. She laughed when she saw it. "I didn't know you had a picture of me."

Mrs. Golden was indignant. "Why shouldn't I? A beautiful granddaughter like you! Why shouldn't I have a picture? I'd like another one of how you look now."

"I'll see if I have a snapshot I can give you," Sophie promised. She looked up at her grandmother shyly. "I was surprised because I thought that when I was a baby. . . . Well, I didn't think you and mother were"—she searched for the right word—"I didn't think you were in touch with each other much."

A pained expression came over Mrs. Golden's bright face. "The past is the past. We all do foolish things in our lives. Your father is a fine man, I love him the way I do my own sons, but I had to get used to the idea. Sometimes

146

it takes a long while to get over the way one is brought up."

"I'm finding that out," Sophie said with a wry smile. "I have to get used to the idea of being Jewish."

Her grandmother gave her a quick hug. "It shouldn't be so hard. You've got lots of good Jewish blood in your veins. Even rabbis in my family. Your mother tells me you can't become a Jew overnight, but I never dreamed I'd have such a *goyish* granddaughter." Mrs. Golden sighed. "It hurts. It's terrible how people drift into a way of life, and the children grow up not knowing anything, not knowing who or what they are."

Mrs. Golden went to her big bureau and took out a small package wrapped in tissue paper. "This is for you," she said, handing it to Sophie. "Open it up."

She watched Sophie eagerly as Sophie tried to take the paper off without tearing it. Putting the paper aside, Sophie found a beautifully hand-stitched little packet made of laced, blue-satin strips of ribbon. It wasn't new, but carefully preserved. Inside the packet was a crisp five-dollar bill.

Sophie kissed her grandmother with delight. "It's lovely. Did you make it? And you're so generous. . . ."

Mrs. Golden was beaming. "I made that for your mother. Every Chanukah she used to get it with five silver dollars inside. Now you can't get silver dollars so easy. I've been saving it all these years, hoping someday I'd be able to give it to you. Mind you, Rachel and Dickie will get their five dollars too—I treat my grandchildren all alike —but that little silk packet is different. I'm a sentimental old lady."

"You're not old," Sophie said spontaneously. "You're a very young grandmother." She ran into the living room to show the packet to her mother, whose face lighted up when she saw it.

"Can I keep it?" Sophie asked her grandmother. "Or do you want it back?"

Mrs. Golden shook her head. "No, no, it's yours now."

Soon afterward they all went in to dinner. The table looked very festive with Mrs. Golden's fine lace table-cloth, her best gold-banded china, and gleaming silver. She served a tremendous meal that included the traditional potato pancakes of Chanukah. As always the talk was voluble and moved easily from one subject to another, ranging from Grandpa Golden's reminiscences of his childhood growing up in New York's lower East Side to an emotional discussion of current politics.

Grandpa Golden addressed his remarks to Sophie, the only one at the table who was hearing his story for the first time. He told her how his father, her great grandfather, had come to this country as a young boy around the turn of the century. He had been smuggled out from his little town in Russia in a vegetable cart to escape the army conscription. Like many immigrants, he came over in the steerage of a boat where the people were packed together like cattle; all his worldly possessions tied up in a small bundle. He did have some relatives in New York, however, and he lived with them on the lower East Side. That's where he met her great grandmother, who had come to this country when she was twelve and began doing piecework at home for the garment industry. "She got the occupational disease, tuberculosis," Grandpa Golden said, "and she died a young woman."

Sophie tried to picture these ancestors of hers, but the only image she could conjure up was one of old men, with skullcaps on their heads and long, flowing beards, and old women wrapped in shawls. She could not think of them as young. Grandpa Golden told of his own youth on the streets of New York, his fights with the Irish boys, how he had once started a fire right out on the fire escape, and how he had had to sit on a hard, wooden bench every afternoon studying Hebrew with a shabby, unkempt rabbi, who had bad breath and smelled of sour wine.

"They were terrible and wonderful times," he said. "There were certain blocks we could walk on, and others where we knew we'd be attacked and beaten up. But still the ghetto in the old country was worse. Here everyone had the hope of getting out and making a pile of money. Some did and some didn't. The German Jews, like your grandmother's family"—he looked at his wife with a smile—"looked down on us. But they got it when Hitler came along."

Long after everyone had finished eating, they sat at the table sipping wine and eating nuts and raisins. "I bet you've never played with a *dreydel*," Grandma Golden said to Sophie. She jumped up from the table to bring a small, filigree silver top to Sophie. "You spin it around," she explained. "You can use nuts or raisins, but we play with pennies. Who has the pennies?"

Grandpa Golden produced a bag of pennies he had brought home from the store. Soon the whole family was engrossed in the *dreydel* game, and Sophie was glad that even Uncle Joe joined in.

Uncle Joe was the first one to leave, and Sophie bolstered up her courage to shake his hand and say that she hoped she could come to visit him one day. He looked surprised, but replied that he would like to see her.

By the time Sophie and her parents left, what with the whiskey and the wine and all the food, she was very sleepy. It was a pleasant, warm drowsiness, and driving home in the snow that made even Woodview look pretty, Sophie felt more at peace than she had since leaving New York.

"I like Grandma and Grandpa Golden," Sophie said to her mother, and was embarrassed by her mother's over-joyed reaction to such a simple remark.

"I suppose things would have been different if you had never left Woodview," Sophie said.

Mrs. Barnes took hold of Sophie's hand between her own two. "I could have done things differently, even in New York. But New York is such an anonymous place, and there had been so many painful scenes. . . . I guess I wanted to forget all about everything, and so we drifted along. I'm not logical about the way I feel. Coming back here and wanting you to prove to my parents that what I did wasn't wrong is all emotional." A half-smile crossed her troubled face. "Perhaps I've been hard on you, but something terrible happens to me when you question your Jewishness. . . . I suppose it's my own guilt."

"I know," Sophie said. She was touched by her mother's unexpected confession, but she knew clearly what she had suspected all along; she couldn't rely on her mother to give her the answers. She was going to have to find out for herself who she was and exactly where she stood.

* * *

151

The next day Sophie left for New York. The minute she entered the old brownstone of her grandparents she was flooded by childhood memories. The same smell of furniture polish, of waxed floors, and of a cleaning deodorant came to her. Had it always been so quiet? Had every piece of furniture been placed so exactly? The *Christian Science Monitor* was folded just so on the hall table, and the window shade was drawn precisely halfway. Her grandparents greeted her warmly, yet Sophie was acutely aware of their shy reserve, her grandmother's peck on her cheek, and her grandfather's handclasp. How long ago had he stopped kissing her?

They sat in what her grandmother still called the parlor, and Sophie answered interested but polite questions about Woodview, school, and the state of her parents' health. Every sentence was grammatically correct and carefully finished, and no one interrupted anyone.

They are such dears, Sophie thought, so gentle and sweet, and yet she felt that something was missing. The house was modestly decorated for Christmas. There was a wreath on the front door, and Mrs. Barnes had a tall vase of holly and leaves at each end of the mantle. A small, beautifully decorated Christmas tree stood in front of a window that reached almost from the floor to the high fourteen-foot ceiling. Charmingly wrapped packages were in place around the tree. The Barnes were ready for Christmas, but the excitement of the holiday was missing.

Everything in this house was done in such a low key that the contrast to the breathlessness at the Goldens' was inescapable. One was formal, the other informal; one was quiet and decorous, the other noisy and full of life. I have never thought this way before, Sophie reflected, even as she went on explaining the courses she was taking to her grandparents.

The remark that one of her parents had made, saying that she had as much Golden blood in her veins as Barnes, came back to her. The idea that she was the product of such a rather marvelous mixture of different cultures was attractive, and it gave her a pleasant sense of being someone special, of having an identity that was unique, hers alone.

Christmas day passed quietly. Sophie had brought down presents from home for her grandparents and she was bringing back gifts from them for her mother and father. The morning was spent opening their packages, and Sophie was delighted with the books and beautiful red sweater that her grandparents gave her. After the big Christmas dinner of roast goose, Sophie and Mrs. Barnes cleaned up the dishes. Then they each retired to their rooms for a rest. Sophie stretched out on her bed, but she didn't want to nap. Being here was nice—she felt warm and safe and secure—yet she could not stop thinking about her two sets of grandparents, comparing their differences and similarities. They were all four fine people —principled, generous, community-minded, affectionate —yet in so many ways they were completely different. They spoke differently, they ate different kinds of food, they behaved differently.

Sophie wondered if the two sets of grandparents had ever met, and she could hardly wait for her grandmother to get up from her nap to ask her. The minute she heard Mrs. Barnes stirring, Sophie went in to talk to her. "I've been wondering if you ever met my other grandparents, the Goldens?" Sophie asked.

Mrs. Barnes's gentle face became guarded. "As you know, there was no wedding. I mean no church wedding. The two of them got married by themselves without any family. But we met later, when you were born. Mr. and Mrs. Golden came to New York. I wanted them to come here, but they took us out to a restaurant instead. They are nice people."

"You don't like them very much, do you?" Sophie was reading her grandmother's face.

"I don't know them well enough to like them or not like

them," Mrs. Barnes said primly. "They were very opposed to the marriage. We did not care that our son was marrying a Jewish girl, but the Goldens carried on so, it worried us." The old antagonisms flared up in her grandmother's eyes. "I'm glad that they feel different now," she added in a measured voice.

"They're crazy about Daddy," Sophie said.

"That is very nice," Mrs. Barnes said, and closed the conversation.

In the afternoon friends from Mr. Barnes's old parish came to visit, and Mrs. Barnes served them apple cider and homemade cookies. I could be in Woodview, Sophie thought, except the conversation would be about different people and different things. What a pity that the two sets of grandparents weren't friends. Sophie believed that they would enjoy each other.

The day after Christmas Sophie told her grandparents that she was going into Manhattan and would probably be gone most of the day. She didn't tell them where she was going, and they were sensitive enough not to ask. She had a plan that had been half forming in her mind ever since she had boarded the train in Woodview. The idea was rather silly, she reflected, while she rode on the subway, but she was curious enough to want to follow it through.

At Times Square she got out of the train and asked the guard how to get to the lower East Side. She followed his directions, taking several subways, and eventually Sophie was on Orchard Street. This street was one that her grandfather Golden had mentioned. She was in the middle of it now, the section of New York where her great grandparents had lived, the Jewish ghetto where her grandparents had grown up. The kosher butcher shops, the pushcarts on the streets, the open stalls that sold everything from dresses and suits to pots and pans and sheets and bedspreads and goods by the yard, everything Sophie had heard described was still there.

Half-frozen old men and women, wrapped in shawls and woolen sweaters, babies with their mothers, young children playing, all were on the streets. Were they all Jewish? Some of the men wore skullcaps and displayed long flowing beards. The neighborhood was a world Sophie had never seen. Noisy, teeming with life on this cold December morning, it showed no signs of the holiday season. There were no discarded Christmas trees on the street and no evidence of Christmas decorations.

Sophie stopped in front of a tiny store that had a sign: *Knishes 5¢*. The smell was rich and inviting, so she went inside and bought a little hot potato cake that she ate with her fingers. It tasted good and she bought another, the woman behind the counter rewarding her with a big smile. Sophie walked in and out of the streets soaking up the sights and sounds and smells until she was tired and cold. She ended up in a huge delicatessen and stuffed herself with a generous hot pastrami sandwich, rich tomato pickles, and a cup of coffee.

As she sipped her coffee she tried to sort out her feelings. Had she thought she would find the answers here? Had she had a romantic notion that she would be coming home to her birthplace?

Ironically, she was the one who was stared at as if she were a tourist. She felt the eyes of the countermen, of the sellers behind the stalls on the street, staring at her as if to say, "What's a well-dressed, tall, slim blond girl like you doing down here by yourself?" They seemed to tag her as an outsider, and their attitude made her angry, made her want to stand up and tell them, "Don't let my looks fool you, I am one of you."

She was shaken by her own reaction. She wanted to walk up to strangers and say, "I have a right to be here, to eat your knishes and pastrami. My great grandparents immigrated here. My grandfather and grandmother grew up in these streets." She did not want to be an anonymous outsider; she wanted to claim her right to belong. New York was the same as any other place. Negroes, Puerto

157

Ricans, Jews, Italians, Irish, all did their own excluding and including, and all endured being excluded by someone else. Sophie knew that there were many clubs and luxury apartment houses that still excluded Jews in New York, and sitting in the grime of the lower East Side the thought filled her with indignation. And yet, she decided, there must be something more than oppression and discrimination that has made these people stick together in this predominantly Jewish community. There must be something positive behind the struggle to remain Jews, and maybe for the first time in her life she was feeling it. Her mother had said it was a tribal feeling, and Sophie could not think of a better way to express it.

When Sophie came home to her grandparents she was shy about telling them where she had been, but she was so full of it she had to talk. Although she was worried that she might hurt their feelings by her sudden interest in the Jewish side of her family, she could see on their faces that they were intrigued. "You have a heritage on both sides of your family to be proud of," her grandfather said.

"I guess I have," Sophie agreed.

XI

A few days later Sophie tried to put into words for Patti's benefit how she felt about her tour of the lower East Side. "Down there I wanted to be Jewish more than when I'm with Shirley Hertzberg or even my Cousin Rachel. I can't explain it; it was odd."

The two girls were stretched out on Patti's bed. Patti's record player was going, but they were not paying attention to the music.

159

"That's because Shirley is a snob. A snob is a snob, Jewish or not," Patti said with finality.

"Do you think that's it?" Sophie was eager to find a reason.

"What about Ricky? Where does he fit into this new-found Jewishness you've discovered?"

Sophie glanced up at Patti quickly. Was she being sarcastic? But Patti's face was serious. "I wish I knew. I don't like that expression, 'new-found Jewishness.' It makes me sound like a phony."

"Aren't you being a little bit phony?" Patti asked frankly. "I mean can you suddenly feel Jewish when you haven't before?"

"I think so." Sophie spoke slowly and deliberately. "Why not? I didn't feel anything before, but I'm beginning to see things differently now. I bet that many Jews in Germany didn't think twice about being Jewish until Hitler came along." She sat up on the bed. "I think I'm going to see my Uncle Joe. He must have a lot of stories to tell."

Patti kept pressing Sophie about Ricky. They were still on Christmas vacation, and Sophie hadn't seen Ricky since she had come back from New York. She hadn't called him, nor did he call her, although she kept telling herself that he probably thought she was still in New

York. "I want to see him," she said to Patti, "but I am not going to call him at home. I couldn't bear it if his mother answered the phone, now that I know how she feels about me."

"You could always hang up," Patti suggested. But Sophie shook her head. She preferred to resign herself to waiting until school opened.

The idea of going to see her Uncle Joe took hold of Sophie, and she could not let it go. The visit would be a continuation of what she secretly and a bit self-consciously thought of as a quest to find her roots. The following Saturday she took her father's car and went in search of Uncle Joe's house. She could not call him because he had no phone, but Saturday she would find him home; he observed the Sabbath.

Sophie drove to the edge of town and after a few wrong turns found a mailbox with the name Joseph Bernstein neatly lettered in black on it. It was at the edge of a path that led to a tiny, freshly painted red cottage. Everything about the place was diminutive but cared for as she could see by the burlap-covered bushes, the gravelled path, and the trimmed hedge. The shabby, old Chevvy that stood in the driveway was almost as big as the house.

Her knock on the door was promptly answered by Uncle Joe. He showed no great sign of surprise at seeing her and welcomed her cordially though with his customary reserve. His house consisted of one room that served as kitchen, bedroom, and living room, plus a tiny bathroom. It was furnished austerely with bare floors and windows, a narrow cot at one end, a few chairs, and a long table which was scattered with bits of small machinery, set up near the kitchen equipment. The room was heated by a large space heater.

"I was just about to prepare lunch," Uncle Joe said gravely. "Would you care to join me? It will be a cold lunch. I do not cook on Saturday."

"I'd love to," Sophie said eagerly. "Can I help you?"

"I think not." A small smile crossed his lips. "You might mix up my dishes. I keep a kosher house."

"Here, all by yourself?" Sophie was surprised.

"Yes, here by myself." Now he smiled outright, making Sophie remember that he once had been a young man.

He pulled out a chair for Sophie and cleared the table of his equipment, carelessly dumping it all into a burlap sack. "I do a lot of things here by myself that I never did before. Hitler made a Jew of me. I go to temple every Friday night too. I never used to when I lived in Leipzig. I thought I was a German then."

Sophie wanted him to go on talking, but she felt shy

162

about asking questions. "What was it like in Germany before . . . before Hitler?" she asked timidly.

Uncle Joe covered one end of the table with a cloth and set out dishes before he answered. "It was a good place to live. I was a young man then, and we paid no attention to politics. Everything was just to have a good time."

Uncle Joe took a plate of chicken and bread from an old-fashioned icebox, and arranged lettuce leaves and sliced tomatoes on a plate. "Come sit down. We can eat."

Sophie pulled up her chair. With a serious face Uncle Joe divided up the chicken pieces evenly, put some salad on Sophie's plate, and handed it to her.

"It's delicious," Sophie said. "You're a good cook."

"I have to be. In the old days I wouldn't have known how to boil an egg. We had cooks and maids and chauffeurs. But they didn't help us any."

"Still, life must have been pleasant then."

"It did us no good," Uncle Joe spoke sternly. "We were stupid and closed our eyes to what was going on. I pray every night that it doesn't happen here in America."

"Do you think it might?" Sophie asked in alarm.

Uncle Joe shrugged. "There is hate and violence. When there is hate you can trust that the Jews will get their share."

Sophie shook her head in bewilderment. "That is one of the things I don't understand. When you got out of . . . out of the concentration camp"—she said the words quickly, because she knew her question involved the one subject Uncle Joe did not ever talk about—"and you came to this country, why did you want so much to be a Jew? I should think you'd rather have been an American or a German."

Sophie was surprised to hear Uncle Joe laugh. "I'll tell you a story," he said. "I have a friend who came over here when I did. He did as you say. He went to a little town in South Dakota, and he joined the Congregational Church. He even became a trustee in the church, and he lived like a Gentile in every way. One day he got a telephone call from the police station. They said, 'Mr. Smith, we have a peddler here who doesn't speak English very well. We can't understand him. He's one of your people. Can you come down here and help us out?'" Uncle Joe laughed again. "You see why?" he asked Sophie.

Sophie smiled with him. "You mean once a Jew, always a Jew?"

"It's in your blood," Uncle Joe said. "I don't say everybody has to do as I do. Not everyone has to keep a kosher house, has to go to services. But for me now the tradition is everything. I want to be the best Jew. I want to show all the little Hitlers that are loose in the world that they cannot destroy us, they cannot break down our faith, our customs, our traditions. We will not give up our ways and accept theirs. They should respect us, they should not discriminate, and they should leave us alone." His thin body was trembling with emotion.

Sophie was afraid she had upset him. "I see what you mean," she said soothingly.

"You see nothing!" Uncle Joe brought his fist down on the table. "I watch you and others like you. You want to be lost in the crowd. You want people to forget you are Jewish, because you want to forget it yourself. But they won't forget, believe me. No one forgets for a minute." He shook his finger at Sophie. "Someday, when you least expect trouble, you will have to face it. Let us hope it will not be in a concentration camp," he warned ominously. "You mark my words."

Sophie was shaken by his vehemence. She tried to put it down to his own horrible personal experience, but his words frightened her.

After Uncle Joe's outburst they did not talk much, and he seemed to be lost in his own thoughts. As soon after lunch as she decently could, Sophie left. Getting out into the clear, cold air after the overheated room, and away from Uncle Joe was a relief. Her visit had been more disturbing than she had anticipated, and only a lot of thought and time, she felt, would prove if the questions in her mind had been answered.

Sophie was eager to get back to school after the holidays, if for no other reason than to see Ricky. She talked to him briefly in class and was happy that he asked her to meet him for lunch.

There was a strain between them when she joined him at a table in the cafeteria. Ricky asked her about her trip to New York, and she told him it had been very quiet. She asked him about his holiday at home, and with a wry smile he said that it too had been very quiet. Then they were both silent and became preoccupied with their food, except for uneasy glances at each other.

Finally Sophie couldn't stand the constraint any longer. "I guess this is the end of a beautiful friendship," she said, trying to make her remark lighthearted.

Ricky shook his head deliberately. "Not for me, it isn't. Of course, if you want to call it quits. . . ."

"That makes me laugh. Your mother's the one who wants us to call it quits, isn't she?" Sophie looked him squarely in the eyes.

"I'll handle my mother," Ricky said gruffly, but his eyes were evasive. Then he turned around and faced her. "I haven't wanted to tell you, but I've been getting some psych counseling. I'm pretty mixed up about my parents and a lot of other things too. My psych counselor thinks I've been using you against my parents. I don't want to do that. I like you, I like you a lot, but I've got to be sure of where I stand. I guess I'm not fit to go with anyone now."

"Don't say that." Sophie was touched by his honesty and his obvious self-disgust. "I'm glad you told me. I'll confess something to you, and you can tell your psych counselor if you want to. I like you too, very much Ricky, but I don't think my falling for the best-looking, blond, Aryan boy in the class was accidental." She put her hand on his arm to soften her words. "This has nothing to do with you. You're a terrific person. It's my problem, not yours."

There was an odd look of relief on Ricky's face. "I guess we both have been using each other. Your telling me that makes me feel better, not quite so small."

"But you're not," Sophie said earnestly. "We shouldn't tear ourselves down."

Ricky grinned. "Yeah, that's right. I guess we're okay."

When Sophie left Ricky she felt as if a great load had been lifted from her. The air had been cleared for both of them. In a way she also felt closer to him, as if they were traveling the same path, side by side, a rocky path that each had to find alone, but along which each could support the other.

XII

Almost spring. The dreary winter days of January and February were receding into a memory of icy roads, snow, and slush. Lots of homework and not much fun for Sophie.

For the Barnes and the Goldens the major excitement was the impending election for the school board. Both sides were working hard, the accusations flying back and forth, and Mr. Barnes was getting progressively more discouraged.

The morning of the election, in early March, Sophie was awakened by a sharp cry. She sat up in bed and realized that her mother had screamed. She ran into her parents' room and found them both in their bathrobes at the window. Her mother was sobbing hysterically.

"What happened? Is Mommy sick?" Sophie was frightened by her father's pale, drawn face and her mother's crying.

Mr. Barnes was holding his wife in his arms and trying to quiet her. "Look out the window," he said to Sophie grimly.

With a pounding heart Sophie went to the window. She didn't know what to expect; had there been an accident? At first she registered only that the snow was gone and the lawn was a hard brown. She saw nothing except some boards sticking up in the ground. Then the significance of the boards dawned on her; they were nailed together into a crude swastika. A note was tacked to the top of it.

A terrible horror and revulsion swept over Sophie. "Who could have done such a thing? What does it say?"

"I haven't gone down to look yet." Mrs. Barnes was sitting on the bed, crying quietly.

"I'll go," Sophie said. She flew downstairs and out into

the cold in her robe and slippers. The air smelled fresh, with a hint of spring in it, and the street was quiet and peaceful. How could anything so sinister have happened here?

The note was written on a page torn out of a lined pad, and the childishly printed words said, "Jew Lover, We Don't Need You in Woodview." Sophie held the paper gingerly with her fingertips as if it were something alive that might bite her. When she came back upstairs, her father was talking on the phone.

When he hung up his face was grimmer than before. "On Harry's lawn too. So far as we know it's just the two of us, them and us." He took the paper from Sophie. "Harry's says about the same thing, except his uses the word *kike*."

"What are we going to do?" Mrs. Barnes turned her tearstained face to her husband.

"Call the police. Probably a bunch of kids thought they were playing a prank," he said to his wife gently.

Mrs. Barnes's face brightened with hope for a moment, and then faded. "No," she said, shaking her head, "you know and I know that it's more than that. It's something organized. Oh, how I wish we had never come to this place!"

"But we did come. And if we weren't involved, Harry

would have been anyway." Mr. Barnes called the police station and told them what had happened. "They'll send someone out to see us. I don't suppose there's much they can do now."

"I feel awful," Mrs. Barnes moaned. "I'm the one who urged you to come up here. I wanted so much to come back to my family. I never dreamed you'd be taking on anything like this when you married me."

"Don't talk that way," Mr. Barnes said sharply. "It doesn't matter whether you're a Jew or a Gentile when it comes to this kind of prejudice! Everyone has to stand up against this filth."

"Daddy, what can I do? I want to do something. To fight back, to pick up a club and hit the offender, to scream out from the housetops that this act was hideous bigotry. . . ." Sophie couldn't bear the inaction.

"I think you'd better get dressed and go to school. There's really nothing we can do," Mr. Barnes said.

Sophie's arms hugged her body in distress. "I can't go to school. I'm going to stay home."

Mr. Barnes put his arm around her. "I think it would be a good thing if you did go. Let's show whoever did this that we can ignore it."

"Do you think so?" Sophie asked dubiously. She was terrified of facing her classmates. Everyone would know, and she felt like someone marked, the way people in Germany must have felt when they were marked with a J.

"You have nothing to be ashamed of. They are the ones who must be ashamed. Anyone in your class who has ever had an anti-Semitic thought should be ashamed today."

"Yes, I know." She stopped and kissed her mother. Mrs. Barnes pulled her down and held her close for a moment. "You're a good girl, Sophie," Mrs. Barnes said.

Sophie could not calm her sense of outrage. She got dressed and tried to eat some breakfast, but without success. She was drinking a cup of coffee when Patti came to the door. Patti's face was stricken.

"You saw it?" Sophie asked unnecessarily.

Patti nodded her head. The next minute she had her arms around Sophie. "Do you want me to take it away?"

"No, we have to leave it until the police come. I feel awful, but I'm glad you came. You're a good friend." Sophie hugged her friend.

"It's the most disgusting thing I ever heard of. But it doesn't represent Woodview. I'm sure only a tiny group can be involved."

"I hope so," Sophie murmured.

Sophie was grateful to be able to go to school in Patti's car. When they arrived they found that word of what had happened already had circulated. Students stood around in small groups talking, and people who had never spoken to Sophie before came up to tell her how bad they felt and how sorry they were that such a thing could take place in Woodview.

Rachel, whose lawn had also been defaced, looked as if she had been crying all morning. "I'm scared," she said to Sophie. "What will they do next?" The Jewish boys and girls hovered together, and many of them did look frightened. "I almost hope my father doesn't win today," Rachel said. "He shouldn't have run."

"But that's wrong," Sophie told her. "He was nominated, and he has a right to run. That's what the others want; they want us to stay in the background and be scared."

Shirley Hertzberg came over to speak to Sophie. "I'm sorry about what happened; we never had anything like this in Woodview before. Maybe it comes from people pushing themselves in where they're not wanted," she said with a humorless smile.

Sophie froze. "Are you insinuating that I provoked this? And my uncle too for running for the school board? That kind of talk makes me want to scream. According to you, everything's all right so long as Jews know their place. Well, their place is the same as anyone else's in this country. I'm sorry if you think that I stirred up trouble. I am a Jew as much as you, but I will not isolate myself and accept discrimination. You'd better examine your own exclusiveness and see what it means."

Sophie walked away bristling, but she was pleased that she had finally put Shirley Hertzberg in her place. Rachel followed her, dumfounded. "I never knew you felt that way about Shirley," Rachel said.

"She may be your friend, but I can't stand her. She's as big a snob as anyone."

"Shirley's ruled the roost around here for so long I suppose we all got used to it." Rachel looked at her cousin with admiration. "I'm glad you told her off. She had it coming to her."

Sophie grinned. "It's the only good thing that's come out of today." While they had been talking she was watching out for Ricky, hoping he would get to school before classes started.

He came running up to her a few minutes before the bell rang. Right in front of everyone he put his arms around her and gave her a sound kiss on the lips. "Sophie, Sophie. . . ." Then he drew her aside and spoke rapidly. "I know everyone thinks my mother is behind this, but I swear she isn't. She wouldn't stoop so low. You've got to believe me, Sophie."

"The thought of your mother never even occurred to me," Sophie told him sincerely.

Woodview once again was the center of the news. Word of the two swastikas brought out newsmen and photographers, and at the closing of the polls the town hall was crowded with people waiting for the results of the election. The people of Woodview were for the most part indignant about the bad publicity their town was getting and disturbed about what had taken place. There were all kinds of speculations, many of them wild, as to who had placed the swastikas, although the police had no clues at all. Sophie heard Mrs. Taylor's name mentioned.

She was with her parents waiting to hear the news, and she told her father that she was sure that Mrs. Taylor had no connection with the incident. Her father agreed. "However," he pointed out, "the position she took gave someone else the impetus. Like bad news, prejudice travels fast."

Sophie had no answer to that criticism. She was frightened by the awful anonymity of the act as she looked at all the faces around her. Maybe someone in that crowd had risen at dawn to drive to their house and to Uncle Harry's. . . . Some sinister person had secretly made those swastikas and written those notes. Who was it? She had a terrible sinking feeling that they would never know, and yet, as her father said, everyone with prejudice was guilty.

Harry Golden strode out of the town hall with the news written all over his long face. He had lost. "The vote was better than two to one," he said grimly. "I really got licked."

That evening the Golden clan gathered at Harry Golden's house. They were a crestfallen group. The vote was analyzed in every way until Sophie thought she would scream if they talked about it anymore.

"With Mrs. Taylor, Stacey, and now Wilfred Parker on the board, I'll finish out the term and quit," Mr. Barnes announced. The others looked at him with dismay.

"I don't blame him," Uncle Harry said. "I'd do the same."

Mrs. Barnes looked unhappy. "But that's giving them what they want. There are others on the board who'll go along with you, Peter. You have to think of the children and their education. Eventually you'll get some of your program through."

Mr. Barnes shook his head uncertainly. "I don't know. I

don't know if I can take fighting every inch." He turned to Sophie. "You at least will be glad if we move back to the city."

Sophie looked at her father thoughtfully. "I wouldn't be here anyway. I'll be away at college most of the year. But I think you ought to stay." Her parents looked at her in amazement.

"I never thought I'd hear you say that!" Mr. Barnes was astonished.

Mrs. Barnes and her mother exchanged glances. "Sophie's beginning to like Woodview," Mrs. Golden cried cheerfully. "It isn't all that bad," she said to her son-in-law.

"I'm not so crazy about Woodview," Sophie said, "but I guess I feel different about other things." She looked around shyly, her eyes returning to her grandmother's face. "I think it would be a good thing for my father to stay here, not to let them drive him out. I think the town has been shaken up, and it can be good for both the Jews and the Gentiles. They both have a lot to learn."

"The kid is right." Grandpa Golden slapped his knee with his hand. "We haven't been so smart. Next time old man Taylor comes into my store I'm going to tell him so too. Why should I give that punk my business when he doesn't want me to join his club? Why should I bow down and thank him for lending me money? I can go into Worcester or Boston to a bank and get money just as easy."

Grandma Golden had an alarmed look on her face, but she supported her husband proudly. "Sure, Sam, you're right."

"Of course, he's right," Helen Golden spoke up in her quiet voice. "We've been accepting anti-Semitism around here for too long, as if it were natural. Who needs it?"

Then everyone started talking at once as they usually did, and what had started out as a defeated, gloomy gathering ended up with plans for the future that were sparked with energy and hope.

When Sophie and her parents left, Sophie felt tired but exhilarated. She sat in front with her father while her mother sat in back. Her father patted her knee lightly. "You're not so sorry now that we moved to Woodview, are you?" he asked.

"As they say," Sophie said with a laugh, "it's been an experience. I guess I've learned a lot. But I wish the Jewish kids in Woodview weren't so snobby."

"They may not all be. Don't judge them all by Shirley Hertzberg. You haven't given them much of a chance," her mother said. "Maybe if you get to know some of them better. . . ."

"Maybe," Sophie agreed dubiously. Even as she was voicing her criticism, Sophie realized that she was speaking as an insider, as one of them, instead of someone from the outside. She never had thought there could be such a difference.

XIII

A few weeks later Sophie was at her grandmother's house helping her get ready for Passover, or Pesach, as her grandparents called it. She was fascinated and overwhelmed by the ritual that Grandma Golden went through. First of all the house had been scrubbed from top to bottom, the curtains freshly laundered, the floors waxed.

But the big job was in the kitchen, and there Sophie

was helping out. Standing on a ladder, she handed her grandmother the special Passover dishes from the top shelf of the cupboard where they had been since the year before. Since the dishes could not touch the *tref* counter in ordinary fashion, every inch of it had to be covered with clean contact paper before a Passover dish could be placed on it.

Grandma Golden was washing the dishes as Sophie handed them to her. "No, no," she cried, as Sophie started on another shelf. "Those are the *milchig* dishes! They're for dairy foods. We're doing the meat dishes now. They have to be kept separate."

"*Oi vey!*" Sophie groaned, jokingly. "I could never keep a kosher house. You have to have four sets of dishes!"

"And four sets of silver too. And pots and pans. I'm telling you whoever invented this must have been in the business," Grandma Golden said with a laugh.

Sophie was enjoying herself with her grandmother. While Mrs. Golden was meticulous about what she was doing, she did not take the idea of it too seriously and was able to laugh at herself. "Spring would not be spring without Pesach," she said. "It's a lot of work, but I enjoy it. The house gets really cleaned! It's a good excuse to have you here with me."

"Who would help you if I weren't here?" Sophie asked.

She came down from the ladder and picked up one of her grandmother's Passover towels to dry the dishes.

"Rachel would come over. Or one of the girls," Mrs. Golden said, referring to her daughters-in-law. "I'm a lucky woman with my girls; they always help. But to have you is a special treat, Sophie. I'll teach you how to be a good Jew."

Sophie laughed. "I'll never go through all this. But I think I can be a good Jew anyway. Aunt Helen and Aunt Sara don't follow this ritual. Neither does Mother."

"They come here instead. But when I'm gone, who will make a Seder?" Mrs. Golden asked with a sigh.

"Someone will," Sophie said cheerfully. "If it's been kept for two thousand years I guess it will go on. But you'll be around for a long time yet," she added. "Who knows? Maybe someday I'll make a Seder."

Mrs. Golden laughed at the idea. "I'd like to live to see that! You and your boyfriend Ricky!"

Sophie smiled. "Ricky's okay. He's a good kid. We're really not going together anymore; we're just good friends. But you know what?" She turned around and faced her grandmother. "I'd like to ask Ricky and my friend Patti to the Seder. Do you think I could?"

Mrs. Golden stared at her granddaughter in astonishment. "Ask them here to the Seder?" Her face was blank.

"Such an idea. . . . I don't know. It's always been just for the family. Why would they want to come to a Seder?"

"I don't know if they want to come. But I'd like to ask them. It's a celebration, isn't it? *They* invite us to *their* celebrations; why shouldn't we invite them to ours. I'm sure neither one of them ever went to a Seder. I think they'd enjoy it."

Mrs. Golden shook her head in amazement. "You're full of ideas!" She shrugged her plump shoulders. "But why not? Ask them. See if they'll come."

"May I?" Sophie was delighted. "Thank you, Grandma. Thank you."

Sophie found herself getting quite excited about the Seder. She had been to only a few herself when she was younger. Ricky and Patti accepted her invitation with pleasure, and she felt that they were coming out of genuine interest and not curiosity. As Sophie had said to her grandmother, she and Ricky had settled down to a calm friendship ever since their conversation in the cafeteria after the Christmas holidays. They saw each other a great deal in school, but except for an occasional movie they did not meet otherwise.

The late afternoon of the first night of Passover, Sophie drove around to pick up Ricky and then stopped for Patti,

184

so that they could drive up to the Goldens together. She was pleased that they had dressed up for the occasion. She felt that she was the hostess for a very special gathering, which gave her an elated sense of worldliness, as if she were guiding friends in a foreign country where she was at home. "Come into my house," was the theme that kept running through her head.

"Good *yom tov*, good *yom tov*." Grandpa Golden was at the door spruced up in his best dark suit, ready to greet them warmly. He shook hands with Patti and Ricky and told them to make themselves at home. Any slight worry Sophie may have had about bringing her two friends into the family circle disappeared after the first few minutes. The Golden clan took them in easily, showing them some deference—"Take a comfortable chair . . . have a little schnapps . . . we'll explain everything to you as we go along . . . we'll slow down Grandpa so he doesn't race through the services"—but at the same time making them feel as if they belonged. Even Uncle Joe broke his customary silence to talk to them for which Sophie was especially grateful.

No one spoke of the lost election or of the school board. And when Aunt Sara asked if there had been any word from the police about the swastikas, Grandma Golden hushed her up. "No talk about that tonight. This is a happy event, and we don't want to be reminded of unpleasant things."

"I hope they find whoever did it," Ricky said quietly. "Everyone in Woodview would feel better."

Sophie's heart beat rapidly during the few seconds of silence that followed, but Grandpa Golden rescued the situation with a jovial smile. "That's right. We'd all feel better, but let's forget it now."

After their drinks and Grandma's wonderful hot *pirogen* (chopped meat wrapped in tiny triangles of flakey pastry dough), the time came to enter the dining room for the Seder.

The table, covered with a fine lace cloth, shining silver candlesticks, the Passover dishes and wine glasses looked beautiful. Sophie sat between Patti and Ricky on cushioned chairs, a tradition since ancient times when reclining at a meal was the mark of a free man. Each was given a Haggadah, the book that had the service with an English translation. Grandpa Golden sat at the head of the table. In front of him was a dish containing three matzohs, covered by the special embroidered cloth used only for this occasion. Two of the matzohs symbolized the two loaves of bread over which the usual prayer was said for the Sabbath; the third matzoh was a reminder of the great haste in which the Israelites fled from their Egyptian oppressors. There had been no time to wait for bread to rise so they had eaten unleavened bread instead.

Also placed before Grandpa Golden was the special large copper plate that had a place for each of the symbolic objects: a roasted shankbone to commemorate the paschal sacrifice brought to the Temple of Pesach in ancient times. A roasted egg to symbolize the *haggigah*, a festival sacrifice; bitter herbs (horseradish) to symbolize the bitterness of Israel's bondage in Egypt; *haroset* (a mixture of grated apples, chopped nuts, cinammon, and a little wine) to symbolize the mortar that the Israelites used to build the "treasure cities for Pharoah"; parsley, lettuce, watercress with a dish of salt water beside it, which symbolized the coming of spring and suggested the perpetual renewal of life.

In addition, there were four cups of wine to be offered during the Seder service, and a special cup in the center of the table known as the Cup of Elijah. In Jewish tradition the Prophet Elijah is the messenger of God appointed to herald the era of the Messiah, an era of perfect happiness when the Jewish people and all peoples throughout the world shall be free.

"Slow down, slow down," Uncle Harry admonished his father. "You're going too fast."

Dutifully Grandpa Golden spoke the words of the service more slowly, stopping often to explain the meaning to their young guests. "This is called the *afikomen*," he explained, as he broke the middle piece of matzoh. "After dinner tonight we shall share it among us."

"Hide it, hide it," his sons chorused.

"We have no children anymore, except for Dickie," Mr. Golden said, patting his grandson beside him on the head. But he got up and followed the custom of hiding the *afikomen* for the children, without troubling really to conceal where he was putting it. "Dickie will find it anyway."

Everyone was quiet as solemnly Dickie, the youngest, finished the ceremony with his grandfather. "We'll eat pretty soon," Sophie whispered to Ricky. "You must be starving."

"No, I'm fine." Both Ricky and Patti were absorbed in the service.

At last the meal was brought to the table, and conversation flowed once more.

When they finally left the dining room, Sophie said she would not be able to eat for weeks. "By tomorrow you'll be hungry," Ricky said.

"I feel stuffed. I need some air." Sophie looked at her mother, and then asked in a whisper if she and Ricky and Patti could go out for a little ride. She didn't think that sitting and talking with the grown-ups would be much fun for them.

"If you take Rachel and Dickie with you," Mrs. Barnes said. "And excuse yourself with Grandma."

Sophie agreed readily and soon the young people were out in the car.

Ricky drove, Sophie and Patti sat in the front with him, and Rachel and Dickie climbed in the back. "You're lucky," Patti said to Sophie thoughtfully. "Having two kinds of families. I mean Christmas and Chanukah and Passover. It must be fun."

"I didn't used to think so," Sophie said, knowing that Patti meant more than the fun of the different sets of holidays. "I'm happy now, though, that I have both, but I think I do understand why my mother doesn't like me to say I'm half-Jewish. It's true, but saying so sounds too much like an apology. No one says he's half-Protestant. You know what?" she said suddenly. "I hate Woodview, but I'm glad I came here. I didn't know anything about America when I lived in New York."

After driving around for a little while Patti asked to be dropped at home, and Rachel tactfully followed her lead. When Sophie was left alone with Ricky, they both remained silent for a while.

"How did you like the Seder?" Sophie finally asked. She

was dying to find out if his parents knew where he had been, but she didn't want to pry.

"I liked it fine. They're great people, all of them."

"The chosen people," Sophie said with a laugh.

"Yes," Ricky said. "One of these days you'll make a good Jew out of me."

"I don't have to," Sophie said soberly. "I don't have to make you into anything, or myself either. I think I'm beginning to understand what it means to be free. There was a lot said about freedom in the service tonight, and it's wonderful to think of the Jews keeping up all these customs for so many hundreds of years in all kinds of places. Tradition seems to help a person know himself and where he belongs, and it makes him proud of himself. Not because he's better than anyone else, but because he's someone in particular. I hope I can hold on to this attitude, remember it when I feel like a bit of nothing."

"You won't remember it," Ricky said philosophically. "Nobody does when he's depressed. But maybe you won't forget it altogether either."

When Sophie said good night to Ricky at his driveway, she was happy to be alone. Riding home through the quiet streets of Woodview, she knew she would be unlikely to feel nostalgic about the town. It had too generous a share of unpleasantness, and yet its very contradictions, its good and its bad, had opened her eyes to both the pain and the pride of being an American Jew.

HILA COLMAN was born and grew up in New York City, where she went to the Calhoun School. After graduation, she attended Radcliffe College. Before she started writing for herself, she wrote publicity material and ran a book club. About fourteen years ago she sold her first story to the *Saturday Evening Post*, and since then her stories and articles have appeared in many periodicals. Some have been dramatized for television. In recent years she has turned to writing books for teen-age girls. One of them, *The Girl from Puerto Rico*, was given a special citation by the Child Study Association of America.

Mrs. Colman and her husband live in Bridgewater, Connecticut. They have two sons, one of whom is married.